A DIAMOND IN THE DESERT

For Mr. and Mrs. Tetsuo Furukawa

⊷•⧓•⊶•○•⊷•⧓•⊶

A DIAMOND IN THE DESERT

Most nights, it's the same dream.

My mind finds a wide Bermuda green field with four white bases. I stand over home plate and see only the pitcher.

I watch through air that shines as if every molecule around me is lit up. I see the white ball leaving the pitcher's fingertips with its seams spinning—a curveball—making its way to my bat.

And then—though this is the part that starts to blur—I feel my arms tighten, and the ball reverses direction away from home plate. I try my hardest to watch where that ball goes as it shrinks into the distance. But the air quickly shatters and breaks apart.

I wake up fast, trapped within the smell of desert sagebrush and gravel, my hands gripped tight to nothing but my own fingernails, and sweat, and Indian dust embedded into the cracks of my palms.

That's when I remember where I am.

August 1942

Gila River
Relocation Center

Rivers, Arizona

GILA RIVER WAS the place where my eight-year-old sister, Kimi, learned to go to the bathroom with a white cotton pillowcase pulled over her head. It was Mama who came up with the idea after a week of Kimi refusing to go.

The pillowcase, Mama said, took the place of the walls and doors that weren't in the latrine, and gave some privacy from others sitting close by trying to use the bathroom, too.

"No one will see you through it," Mama promised. "Yes, you'll be able to breathe. The air can get in."

Then she stood for three long minutes with the pillowcase over her own head to prove this.

"But what if it takes me *more* than three minutes in the latrine?" said Kimi.

Mama didn't answer. Instead, she pulled the pillowcase back over her head, sat down on the concrete floor, knees bent, shoulders curled in. Stayed there until the desert bats came out and the sky turned dark orange.

Kimi walked a circle around her, and you could see her deciding that this idea might work.

"Can you still breathe?"

And each time Kimi asked, Mama nodded. But I don't think Mama was taking all that time to show Kimi she could breathe. I think Mama was hiding the sadness she didn't want Kimi to see.

GILA RIVER WAS a place where my dog, Lefty, couldn't come.

After Executive Order 9066 was issued, ordering all persons of Japanese ancestry to internment camps, our neighbor drove Mama and me and Lefty ten miles away to Mr. Nestor's strawberry farm, where dogs were boarded. I had to *give him away*, because that's what was best for Lefty. Because internment camps don't take dogs. Because a strawberry farm is a good place for a dog while his owner can't take care of him. It took Lefty only one day before he ran away from that farm.

Mr. Nestor's letter came late. I got it after we'd already been moved from the horse stall we had lived in at the Tulare Fairgrounds Assembly Center while the government decided what was next for Japanese Americans. People were suspicious of anyone who was Japanese after those pilots from Japan bombed Pearl Harbor. It didn't matter that we'd lived here our whole lives or that we were American citizens.

The letter was forwarded to me: Tetsu Kishi, Butte Camp, Block 28-12-B, Rivers, Arizona. Mr. Nestor said he was sorry, but all that remained of Lefty was the T-shirt I'd taken off with my scent on it so I could make a bed for my dog.

It's better I didn't get that letter sooner. It's better I had pictured Lefty on that strawberry farm all this time. Because when I read that letter to Mama and Kimi, Mama bent her head down and glared at the dust on our floor that'd found its way back into our barrack since yesterday's sweeping.

Then she stood up and swept harder than I'd ever seen her sweep a floor.

And Kimi said, "Lefty's making his way back to our old house."

And we all agreed that's what he was doing.

For the rest of the day, we reminded each other that Lefty was going home. And it was enough to keep us moving.

But I kept thinking that when Lefty got there, I wouldn't be there to fill his water dish or take the thorns out of his paws that he'd get when he ran through the boxwood along the highway. I wouldn't be there to pull foxtails from his fur.

It was Kimi who taught Lefty to shake, after Papa brought him home, five pounds of short-haired black-and-white spots, a country mutt. No matter how many times she tapped his right paw, he lifted his left. Because he was a lefty.

I told Kimi he was like Lefty O'Doul, left fielder, left-handed batter, left-handed thrower.

Nothing anyone can do to change a lefty.

GILA RIVER WAS a place where you heard people you didn't know breathing at night. And if they started snoring, there was nothing to do but cover your ears and try to ignore it. Or hurry and fall asleep before they did.

But there's a lot of noise that comes through thin walls.

And even though Mama reminded Kimi and me to mind our manners, to be polite and not eavesdrop, we couldn't help but hear when the newly married couple next to us argued about their belongings they had to give away for hardly any money to a Caucasian man named Leonard.

Or when, much later, they went to bed having forgiven each other their harsh words and . . . you know.

GILA RIVER WAS a place where summer came in March, and black scorpions crawled into your shoes at night to hide.

It was a place where dust devils swirled like small tornados sending broken pieces of saguaro into the sky a mile high, and weedless, burned dirt somehow grew sagebrush, hiding black, shiny arrowheads buried beneath sacred Indian territory.

And when I got there, it was a place where barbed wire stretched in twisted jumbled coils to remind us of what had happened on December 7, 1941.

Gila River was where I would turn thirteen, and live with my mama and my sister, while waiting for my papa to be brought back from Fort Lincoln, North Dakota, where the FBI had sent him so they could find out more about him after Pearl Harbor was bombed.

BEFORE WE WERE brought to Gila River, my parents were dirt farmers, growing lettuce, broccoli, and artichokes, on two hundred acres of rented West Coast land.

Papa taught me to hoe the weeds, and when I was ten, to drive the tractor. He spoke mostly Japanese but learned some English while working the sugar fields in Hawaii, where he saved enough money to make passage to California for him and Mama.

Mama spent her days helping at the church, baking mostly. Papa grew crops from soil no one else could farm and made furniture from scrap lumber for Mama. He couldn't read or write English, but he built me a batting cage where I would hit the balls he threw after all the weeds were pulled.

He'd tell anyone who'd listen how I was gonna be the greatest hitter ever, and my batting average would break 400. He'd say this like he had no doubt, and people should be lining up for my autograph because it'd be worth a lot someday.

I BECAME A good hitter, with a .324 average. I was known for my hard line drives between short and third. I became a good first baseman, even though I wasn't a lefty. I was team captain of the city league by the time I was twelve.

MAMA HAD ONE month to pack up our house before they bused us to the Tulare Assembly Center. But she wasn't sure what to do without Papa there to tell her. We knew that the government had arrested him because he was so involved in the Japanese community. Papa was the superintendent of the Japanese Association, a consultant to the Japanese Farmers' Association, and on the board of our church. Like most people in our neighborhood, we were used to looking up to him.

So I did everything I could in his absence. I tried to see things through Papa's eyes and sell only the furniture we couldn't store.

Papa couldn't send us a letter from North Dakota, where the government had sent many of the men they arrested. He didn't know how to write in English. No Japanese writing was allowed anymore.

We couldn't say, *No, we're not leaving,* because just about everyone—even Marty Burns, the shortstop on my team that I'd known since first grade—their faces said:

> *I can see you're Japanese. And those pilots who bombed Pearl Harbor, maybe one of them is your brother or your uncle—how are we supposed to be sure? You've got no choice but to leave, because we're not buying your papa's crops or letting him head up our community. We're not letting you play first anymore.*

If you saw their faces, you'd know what I mean. You'd pack your two bags like they told you to. Two bags to hold your whole world.

I gave Mama the space in my two bags, so she could bring her grandmother's wedding dishes.

But Mama said, "*Please*, Tetsu, pack your things."

So I went to my bedroom that Papa had painted blue and where he had hammered shelves up above my bed for my baseballs and my books about baseball. And I saw myself sitting on my bed. It was my little self. Papa was telling me a story before bedtime about a mouse. We were laughing about that mouse, and no one had dropped a bomb.

I folded pants and shirts, one coat, and some socks, all into a neat pile on my bed.

But when I came out, I handed Mama the only thing I cared about taking.

My Mel Ott baseball glove.

THE MORNING WE boarded the Greyhound bus for the Tulare Assembly Center, I sat on the steps of our house waiting to leave. I tried to make my face look as brave as I could, mostly for Mama's sake.

My teammate Harold came over. He played right field.

"I came to say good-bye, Tetsu," he said. "Take care of yourself. Keep up your batting practice."

"Don't think there's baseball where I'm going," I said. My voice sounded like I was someone else.

Harold stood around a while longer, kicking at the dirt, and you could see on his face how bad he felt about everything.

"I heard on the radio that all major league ballparks will play the 'Star Spangled Banner' before each game now," he said, real cheerful. "They used to only play that song before World Series games or on opening day."

I thought about why my family was being forced to leave everything.

I thought about that "Star Spangled Banner."

How the song said it was waving over the land of the free and the home of the brave.

WE WERE AMONG the first to be moved from the Tulare Fairgrounds Assembly Center in California to the Gila River Internment Camp in Arizona by the government. I was happy to leave that horse stall. No matter how much Mama and I cleaned, it still smelled like horse droppings. Living there made us feel like we didn't belong in our own country.

On the bus to Gila River, you could see how people didn't know what came next.

The boy across the aisle about my age gripped a small, black bag in his lap, and I was sure everything he still owned was in that bag. He looked at me once an hour after we left, but in his eyes, no one was there.

WHEN WE FINALLY arrived in Gila River, Mama stepped off the bus ahead of us. Trying to make the best of it, to not complain, the way she'd been raised, the way she worked to raise us, she picked up a handful of dirt.

"This land looks like virgin soil," she said. "Papa wouldn't need fertilizer here."

And sure enough, there was already a farm going, tended to by evacuees from other assembly centers who'd gotten there before us. Vegetables mostly.

There were two camps in Gila River—Butte, which was ours, and Canal, three miles east. Someone said Canal Camp had a U.S. soldier guarding it, but I didn't see any in Butte.

We found our barrack, 28-12-B, and moved in. It didn't take long.

Then Mama swept the dust out of our twenty-by-twenty-four-foot room and hung a sheet for privacy to make a sleeping area. And she never said anything about what we left behind, or how we were supposed to live with a sheet for a wall. She just sent me for straw to fill the mattresses because the newly married woman next door to us told her that's what I should do.

On my way there, I walked through rows of rectangular-shaped housing that all looked identical, for over ten thousand Japanese American evacuees. I was walking through piles of lumber and crowds of people standing around, through dust and glare and new faces, when I heard a group of three boys about my age. They were planning to crawl through the barbed-wire fence behind block 67 and walk to the canal where water trickled through a dirt trench.

When they saw me listening, one of them asked, "You wanna come? It's forbidden land. Meet us after dinner."

I shook my head and made my way for straw.

"You scared?" they yelled.

I kept walking, picked up my pace, wondering if the camp administrators knew about the space in the barbed-wire fence behind block 67.

KIMI CAUGHT A lizard, four inches long, tumbleweed colored. She put it in a small cardboard box with a handful of dirt and a lid over the top.

When she saw me walking back, carrying the pile of sunburned prickly straw to stuff in our mattresses, she held the box out to me.

"This is Yoshi," she told me. "He's a lefty, too."

"How can you tell?" I asked.

Kimi looked at me with those eyes that always found the good part of things.

"I can tell," she said.

IT TOOK A while to get used to the water and the food at Gila River. The smells in the mess hall weren't like any from Mama's kitchen. Nothing that made me want to wash my hands or sit down with a napkin in my lap. My stomach couldn't get it right, all blocked up and on edge.

The rice was fine, I guess, but most of the meat made me sick. So sick that one night, after waiting hours outside our block 28 latrine, watching for a time when no one else was there from the fourteen barracks surrounding it, which was fifty-six families assigned to the same bathroom, I finally decided it was better to make my way behind block 67. That way, I could crawl through the space in the barbed-wire fence to find a spot in the desert where I could be alone.

Didn't matter how far away block 67 was.

Didn't matter how scared I was to crawl through that fence.

There are times you need to be by yourself.

IT WAS PRETTY easy to crawl through that barbed-wire fence. There was no one around to see. Only Japanese American guards, who sometimes turned their heads in mercy. And soon, I got in the habit of waiting till nighttime to crawl through the fence and find a spot behind a bush so I could go to the bathroom by myself.

And at first I'd walk out to that desert like I was just looking around, and I wasn't doing anything wrong, or wasn't where I shouldn't be. Then I noticed a boy one night. He was walking with a roll of tissue in his left hand, and I'd never seen him before, but I felt like I could be his friend.

THE FIRST TWO weeks in Gila River went by while we tried to set a routine of sweeping out the dust, and eating, sleeping, and talking to our new neighbors. Most of them were from California, too.

I did chores for Mama around our barrack. I swept before she asked me to. I swept and told her:

Everything will be okay, Mama. See how clean the floors are now? What else can I do for you, Mama? Why don't you sit down?

And I could see that it made her feel better, so I'd tell her again, I'd lie and say everything will be okay, and my face showed I meant it.

I looked for things to do since I had no school to go to, no baseball team, no weeds to pull, no Papa to tell who I'd tagged out on a leadoff.

At night, Mama, Kimi, and I would make our way to dinner early so we'd avoid the long lines outside the mess hall. But one night, we heard an unfriendly wind and smelled the earth in the air.

We looked past the barbed wire, and that's when we saw it. A blur of brown moving toward us. For a minute, we stood watching, because we'd never seen a brown wall of clouds moving so fast, so angry.

The sky turned from bright white blue to dark brown, like someone was scribbling brown crayon as fast as they could on paper.

"Dust storm coming!" yelled the man next to us.

Mama told us to turn back to our barrack, to forget about missing the long lines.

Inside, we tore a sheet Mama had brought from home as quickly as we could. We stuffed it into the cracks in the floor and the walls, everywhere, to keep that dust from coming inside.

Didn't matter.

Nothing anyone could do to keep out dirt when it made up its mind to become a dust devil.

GRIEF LIVED AT Gila River. It collected in barracks and mess halls and latrines. It was there in Mama's face late at night when she thought I wasn't looking.

We walked around it cautiously, like it was a spiked saguaro cactus, bulky arms twisted high, extended on all sides.

We didn't speak of its sharp thorns or its long roots anchored tight to nearby jagged rocks.

23

TWO BROTHERS MOVED in next to us, with their mama *and* their papa, into the A section of barrack 12, block 28.

One older than me. One younger than me.

When the older one met me, he asked, "You play any baseball?"

Before I had a chance to answer him, the look on my face must've told him I did. Because he nodded real slow, in a way that said "good."

TURNS OUT, THE brothers in A, their papa was a baseball coach. A real coach who played real ball before he came here.

The older brother, whose name was Kyo, and the younger brother, whose name was Ben, played together on an all-star team before they came here.

I could sort of tell by the way they threw to each other.

Kyo wore an old Yankees cap that looked like it'd been through a hundred baseball seasons. He had eyes the color of scorched wood; he was skinny and tall, same as me.

"The 1942 World Series started today," he told me.

He thought New York would win easy 'cause they had Joe DiMaggio.

He threw the baseball to his brother, showed off a little the way he threw so hard.

"You got a glove?" he asked me.

"Yeah, I got a glove," I told him.

"You wanna play catch?" asked his brother, Ben. He had short black hair that stuck out like coarse wire.

I smiled and told them yes. Told them I had a Mel Ott. And I could see they were happy I lived next door and this was something we'd be doing a lot of.

After I ran as fast as I could to get my glove, Kyo threw to me like Marty Burns used to. Like a shortstop throwing to first trying to beat the runner. Kyo threw to me, and I threw to Ben, and a cloud of dust exploded from our mitts each time we caught that ball.

And it didn't matter about the 117-degree heat, or that we hadn't played on the same team before. Playing catch felt like everything I'd left behind, and Gila River disappeared for an hour.

Fall 1942

I **WAS WALKING** to the barbed wire behind block 67 after dinner one night, earlier than usual, when I saw that same group of boys I'd seen my first night.

"Where are you going?" the oldest one asked me.

He smirked and showed me a broken front tooth. He looked like the fighting type.

"Nowhere," I said.

He squinted at me, spit in the dirt by my shoes, and the dust swirled up behind him like it was getting out of his way.

"You're coming with us to the canal," he said.

I turned back toward camp and took three steps, when he grabbed my arm, not hard, but firm.

"You're coming with us," he said very clear, while three sets of eyes dared.

So we crawled through the fence with me flanked on either side.

"They must know people come through here," I said.

And the oldest one, he said—like I didn't know anything—
"You think they *care*? There's no place to run to. Where are
we gonna go? We're on an Indian reservation in the middle
of nowhere." He shook his head, and I decided to keep quiet.

I kept thinking I'd make a run for it, but at the same time,
I wanted to see what was out there, and I had nothing else
to do. They said they were gonna get a pomegranate tonight.
That they were gonna be the first ones, and Ralph Omura
wasn't gonna beat them to it. Because next thing you knew,
Ralph Omura would be showing off and telling people where
they couldn't sit in the mess hall.

We hiked for miles through sagebrush and prickly pear
and yucca, over shiny bits of gravel and dirt and rounded-
out snake holes carved into earth. I hoped Mama wouldn't
miss me, and started making up a story about how I'd taken
a long walk around the camp to explain why I'd been gone.

"You think he'll be there?" one of them asked the others.

"He'll be there," the oldest one told him.

I smelled the water before I saw it. It was out of place in
the desert, carried in from far away, trickling through a deep
dirt trench.

We stopped at the edge of that canal, across from a line
of shacks decaying from wind and desert sun. Across from
a row of pomegranate trees sixteen feet tall with spiny

branches, the kind with suckers growing out from the base that no one had tended to. Their leathery red fruit looked like precious stones.

We watched the black-brown mud water swirl below while our feet pushed crumbling dirt clods into the flow.

A catfish splashed, broke the quiet.

"Give me the pennies. I'll make the deal," the oldest one said to the others. His black hair stuck out in tangled clumps, looked like he hadn't combed it in years.

Then he yelled out a whoop that carried into the sky.

After a minute, an Indian came out from a shack. He was older than we were, with hair blacker than ours and past his shoulders. He walked to the opposite edge of the canal, three feet from us, and looked us over hard.

The oldest held out his hand, showed a stack of copper pennies that matched the color of the ground. You could see it on his face, how he was gonna be the first to get a pomegranate, and no one was gonna tell him where to sit.

The Indian waited.

And the boy reached his hand out farther, over the canal water. "Pomegranates," he said.

The Indian nodded and walked toward the trees. He grabbed hold of an angular branch, and picked pomegranates.

"See?" said the boy. "I knew it would work."

He smiled, showed his half tooth, nodded proudly. He was seeing himself with those pomegranates when his foot slipped, and the dirt beneath him gave way into the black-brown mud water.

I stepped back, afraid.

His friends quickly grabbed his shirt.

His legs splashed wildly, kicking and struggling to find their way to the side. Then his shirt ripped and he fell into forehead-high water.

Right away we all knelt down on the crumbling dirt edge and reached our hands out to him. The Indian ran for a stick.

Water swirled around him, pushing him two feet to the right as he swallowed dirty mouthfuls and coughed.

Somehow, it was *my hand* he found. His fingers anchored so tight around mine that I thought he might pull me in, too.

But the others held me down while I worked to pull him up.

"Hold on!" I yelled.

When he finally lay next to me on dry ground, he rested his head on tiny bits of gravel, which stuck to his wet face.

He slowly opened his other hand to only one penny. He looked at the penny, and then over to me, and his eyes, they were different from before.

"Here," he told me. "You have it."

"It's okay," I said, and quickly stood up.

He stood up, too, scraped wet mud off his pants and out of his shoelaces.

Told the others, "Let's go." Told me, "I'm George."

We left in a hurry. I was walking next to George, and the Indian was standing on the edge of the canal with his pomegranates still in one hand and a stick in the other.

Just after we walked past the bluff where the tall saguaros stood, George turned to me.

"Thanks for pulling me out," he said.

I knew it meant that he was now my friend, and there'd be no more spitting in the dirt at my shoes or yanking my arm. And it made me, for just a minute, miss Papa a little less.

SEEMS KYO MIGHT be right. New York won the first game of the series against St. Louis, 7-4.

"My father knows someone who gets the scores and reports them in the *Gila News-Courier* they print here at camp," said Kyo. "You can go to the recreation barrack and get a newspaper and see for yourself if you want."

"We'll let you know what happens in the next game, though," said his father, smiling. "Just in case you don't get over there."

He put his hand on my shoulder when he told me this, like I was his son, and we were on our way to the batting cage on our farm after all the weeds had been pulled.

I stood next to him feeling his hand there, and I thought how it must be good to have a papa around.

MAMA SAID THEY'RE looking for teachers. And that many of the adults want to start up a school for all of the children who haven't been attending any classes since they left home. She said it'll be as close to a regular school as they can make it.

They just need paper, pencils, books, desks, and teachers.

Mama's thinking of getting a job in the mess hall. She's used to cooking for lots of people, like she used to at our church. And it pays sixteen dollars a month. She said she's tired of sweeping out dust all day and worrying about Papa.

She said that she's not used to so much time on her hands, and that we could use the money.

She said it'll be my job then to walk Kimi to the latrine while she's at work. And not to forget the white pillowcase.

KIMI CAUGHT ANOTHER lizard today. She put it in the same box with Yoshi, and a second handful of dirt.

"I'm looking to catch a Gila monster now," she said.

"Be careful," I told her. "They're poisonous, like rattlers."

"But they're so colorful and pretty. Plus, they're slow. I could catch one easy."

"They're not pretty," I said. "They're dangerous."

"No more dangerous than you sneaking through the fence every night," she said.

I SAW KYO in the mess hall.

"The Yankees were shut out in game three of the series," he told me, and on his face, the world had ended. "They're behind two games to one."

"They'll come back," I said.

Kyo took off his Yankees hat and looked at it a minute. Then he turned and walked out the door without answering or getting any dinner.

MAMA TOLD ME, "They've found a principal for your school. And two Caucasian teachers so far who were contracted by the government for the positions. People say those two teachers volunteered to come all the way out here. They're getting more. At least it's a start.

"You won't have many books to use yet," she said. "But they're cutting cardboard squares and drawing a keyboard on them with a pen so everyone can practice their typing skills in the meantime."

Mama said this like she expected that very soon we'd leave Gila River and a typewriter would appear just so I could show how far my typing skills had come, and I'd get a good job because of it, and wasn't I lucky to have those cardboard squares.

I STOOD AROUND one afternoon while Mama was at work, the only man outside the ladies' latrine, waiting forever for Kimi.

Mama babies her.

Kimi could come here by herself.

She could carry her own pillowcase.

But when I decided I'd had enough stares, and walked back to our barrack, Kimi ran to find me.

"Where were you? Where *were* you?" she cried.

KYO PLAYED CATCH with me outside our barrack the next day. I didn't tell him it was my birthday.

"The series is almost over and New York is behind. If they lose game four today, and the Cardinals win game five, it'll be the first time since 1926 that they don't win a World Series they've played in," Kyo said. He hurled the ball into my mitt, and asked what position I played.

"First," I told him, throwing it back harder. "You?"

"Catcher," he said. "Ben plays third.

"You a good hitter?" he asked, throwing it to me again.

"I'm okay," I said, but I knew Papa would tell it different. "I wasn't on an all-star team, but I hit it hard enough to get on base most times." I threw him a high fly back.

Kyo nodded and tossed the ball in the air like we knew all we needed to about each other, and the dust started up between us.

"Good," he finally told me. "We need a guy like that."

THAT NIGHT, LYING on my cot, with the heat making it too hard to sleep, and the sheets scratching my skin, and my stomach aching from dinner, I smiled even still, because Kyo said he needed a guy like that.

"I'm sorry I didn't have a present for you this year," said Mama as she got into her cot.

"That's all right, Mama," I told her. "I had an okay day."

THE FIRST DAY of school, the thermometer read 100 degrees before breakfast. I went early to see the teacher who'd volunteered to come all the way out to Gila River.

I walked Kimi to the third-grade barrack, then found mine, which was eighth grade. The teacher smiled when she saw me there so early, told me to come inside the room. She dropped her book and smoothed her flowered skirt a lot while we waited for the others. I didn't know what to do, either.

Kyo was in my grade.

Ben was one year behind us, and George was one year ahead. I saw him pass by our door with his broken front tooth that would make most teachers put him up front.

When everyone else got there—at first it was only nine of us, with our clean clothes and our hair just so—the teacher read from a book of poetry while we listened.

I had a hard time keeping still and remembering everything she read.

I had a hard time being inside again, but wanted to show her I was once a good student.

I had a hard time forgiving those rough wood walls that were supposed to be a classroom.

But she said, "Don't worry. There won't be any tests for a while. We still need paper."

MAMA WANTED TO know why I didn't go to dinner at the mess hall with her and Kimi anymore.

"Because," I told her carefully, "no one here my age sits with their parents. They sit with their friends."

Mama frowned and clutched that broom like she had enough strength to sweep the dust out of a hundred more barracks.

"There's no discipline here," she said. "Your father wouldn't like all these gangs of boys running around unsupervised."

And I could see she was mad about much more than where I sat at dinner. But she'll have to get in line to file her complaint behind the lady whose children have to share a cot, and the family whose grandfather somehow got separated from them.

"I'm sorry, Mama," I said. "That's just what everyone does."

Mama shook her head. Then she turned her back while I slipped out the door to meet Kyo and Ben for dinner.

I FOUND KYO'S younger brother, Ben, sitting outside the recreation barrack one day after school. I sat down next to him.

"Kyo refuses to play catch today," Ben said. "He won't even come outside. Wanna get your glove and it'll be just the two of us?"

"Yes," I told him, and then ran to get it.

We threw the ball back and forth for over an hour. Ben didn't throw as hard as Kyo, but he threw straighter, like a pitcher hitting the strike zone every time.

Ben didn't like the Yankees as much as his big brother. Said not to tell him, though.

He liked night games best. Said the government wasn't allowing them anymore, though, at least not while the war was going on. The lights over the field could aid an enemy attack.

Just about the time my arm got tired, and he'd told me everything about himself, he said, "New York lost the series,

4-2. Kyo wishes someone would've been on base when Phil Rizzuto hit his homer. Then maybe they would've scored more."

We sat down in the dust, kicked at rocks wedged under the dirt, and quietly mourned the loss of the Yankees, and night games, and everything else we used to have.

That day, playing catch didn't seem to help like usual.

Winter 1942

"MY PAPA'S THINKING of making a baseball field," Kyo told me one day.

I looked at him, surprised, then knelt down in the dirt.

"How's he gonna do that?" I asked.

"He's designed ball fields before," Kyo said.

He pointed to the desert outside the barbed wire, next to block 28.

"He says there's enough room out there. He thinks the camp administrators will give him permission, because baseball will give people something to do while they're here. It's gonna take a lot of work getting the area cleared. You wanna help?"

I walked toward the fence and grabbed tight to the dusty metal. Noticed how November still looked like summer in the Arizona desert.

I pictured home plate, and the dust rising off the batter's shoes as he made his way around third, and the baseball soaring past center, and the look on the catcher's face.

I heard the yells from the crowd, and the ump hollering, *Safe!*

"I can help," I told Kyo, like each word was sweet cake on my tongue.

MAMA TOOK KIMI to a church service on Sunday morning at ten o'clock. She made a big to-do, wore her best clothes, and sang the Japanese song "Yuyake Koyake" while brushing Kimi's hair. She even put on her ivory bird brooch to make Kimi feel as though it would be like back home.

But I didn't go.

Instead, I sat in our barrack and picked at my dirty fingernails and wondered how my papa was, all the way in North Dakota.

I thought about setting Kimi's lizards free, in case they wanted to leave this place as much as I did.

I sat in our barrack because I didn't think it would help much to pray.

AT SCHOOL, OUR teacher couldn't wait to tell us that two hundred books had just arrived in the community library barrack, and they could be checked out to read.

She had us vote on which one we wanted her to get first so she could read it aloud to us.

She told us what some of the books were about, and how she had read them before, with eyes that looked like Papa's the day I told him I made captain of the baseball team.

And for a minute, she looked like a regular teacher standing in front of us, and we were a regular class inside a regular classroom with pencils and books and an apple on her desk, and everyone had all A-pluses, and there was no war going on forcing us out here.

And at the end of the day, the bus would drive up, and take us all home. For a minute, that's what it was like while she counted hands.

For a minute.

GILA RIVER GOT so cold in December that Kimi climbed into bed with Mama at night.

"Pretty soon, we'll get oil-burning stoves installed," Mama whispered. "And you'll be warm again."

The next day, I went to school late. I walked around and looked for all the scrap lumber I could find. I carried armloads back to our barrack that night so I could make a small fire outside, and we could feel its warmth. And to show Mama that I can be like Papa.

I can make something out of scrap lumber, too.

I DIDN'T EXPECT any kind of gift for Christmas, but I got one, and it was big enough to share with Mama and Kimi.

It was a letter from Mr. Bobkin, our neighbor in California. He wrote about his crops doing well. He wrote about his new brown horse that his wife named Red. He went on about the weather being colder than last year.

And he told us he saw a *dog* roaming around his farm last week out by his post fence, where his 150-year-old California oak stood.

He said it looked a little like Lefty. Only it couldn't have been Lefty, he wrote, because this dog had only one good eye, and looked pretty banged up.

I read that letter to Mama and Kimi thirteen times. I read the whole thing, again and again. Mama and Kimi listened so quiet; they wanted to hear the part where Mr. Bobkin saw a dog that looked like Lefty.

Later, I let Kimi fold that letter into a tiny crane and hang it above her straw mattress with string. It swayed in the draft that came through the cracks in our walls.

And after only one day, it'd collected enough dust to make it look old and forgotten.

But my mind imagined Lefty sleeping under that California oak so much that I wondered how there was room for anything else.

KYO ASKED IF I wanted to play catch. He already had his mitt on. He knew I'd say yes.

"I've invited some other guys," he said. "I'm hoping to put together a team for the field we're gonna make."

He leaned against the barrack, watching for the others to show up. Anyone with a mitt would've been fine.

"I'm not sure if they're coming or not," he said after a few minutes.

"We can wait a while longer," I told him.

"They may not be the best players," he said.

"They don't have to be the best," I said.

And we both nodded, and watched some more, and hoped someone would come. Someone who could play second or left, or had his own bat even.

And I decided, while I was standing there next to Kyo, that baseball was like that.

It made you wait around for anyone with a mitt to show up.

THE LATRINES RAN out of toilet paper. And the administrators had to call for conservation of tissue.

Kimi said, "How am I going to do that?"

"It's just like everything else around here," Mama told her. "Less."

I RAN INTO George after school. He could hardly slow down long enough to talk.

"We're going back to the canal tonight," he said. "We're gonna get those pomegranates before Ralph Omura does. I heard him say he was going tomorrow after school. You wanna come with us?"

I thought about it. Shifted from foot to foot. Pulled a loose string from my shirt. Finally told him, "Yes."

KIMI GAVE ME a small scrap of paper to send back to Mr. Bobkin. She said she'd been working on it that afternoon, and that her teacher had helped her with it.

It had only two lines:

> Please feed Lefty.
> From, Kimi.

I took it to the recreation barrack and asked around for an envelope. Someone was showing off their model airplane collection.

But no one had an envelope. So I put it in my back pocket carefully, for later, for when there was an envelope around.

AFTER DINNER THAT night, Mama and Kimi went to bed to get warm.

I found the gray coat I'd brought, and buttoned it up to my neck. Said I was going for a walk.

I took my time getting to block 67, walked slow enough, sort of hoped I'd miss them.

When I got there, George stood up from the cold, packed gravel and wiped dust off his pants.

"Where've you been?" he said. "We've been waiting."

I shrugged, told him, "Let's go."

After we crawled through the fence, George pointed to his little brother. "This is Zuke," he said. "He's an okay sumo wrestler, I guess."

Zuke was a big, round guy with a face that matched and small black eyes you had to search for. He told George, "I'm a lot better than you are. You want me to prove it right now?"

George ignored him and pointed to a guy with massive broad shoulders and even bigger feet. "This is Horse," he said. "Horse never talks to no one, so no need for you to try."

Horse didn't say anything.

And then, like he'd almost forgotten the part I'd want to know most, George said, "Zuke played center field for his baseball team last year."

I nodded to them both, then looked Zuke close in the eye. He seemed like he missed fielding as much as I missed catching the ball at first.

George said he knew the way to the canal, even in the dark.

We walked together over newly formed sand dunes sculpted by desert wind, past a barrel cactus that looked like a giant pineapple, which George said we could drink the insides of if we ever got lost in the desert.

"See these two saguaros?" George stopped suddenly and pointed to the cacti. "The tall ones with three arms. They gotta be fifty years old. Maybe even a hundred."

The four of us bent our necks upward, nodded together, agreeing.

"Maybe two hundred," said Zuke.

"They sure got a lot of needles," I said.

And Horse, he didn't say anything. But according to George, this was normal.

We paid our respect, then made our way again.

We walked by a bluff and saw a lone, gray coyote on top. He was the size of a small ranch Labrador, all shabby and hunched over with his head hung low like he might be hungry enough to come after us.

It was Zuke who yelled unexpectedly. He stopped us in our tracks, pointing to his thigh.

"Something bit me!" he cried.

George bent over his leg and looked real close while we circled around, squinting to see.

"Naw," George said. "It's only jumping cactus."

"Pull the thorns out," Zuke told him. "Hurry up!"

"You can't walk too close to the chollas," George told him. "They'll leave needles hanging in your clothes. Plus they're hard to pull out because of their barbs."

Zuke didn't seem like the whining type, with his sumo-wrestling threats and all, but he whined the whole time while George pulled thorns from his brother's pants and the bottom of his jacket; and how was he supposed to know about the chollas, he kept asking.

"I can't go on," Zuke told us after most of the thorns were removed. "My leg aches."

He sat in the dirt and held his knees to his chin, while his breath formed stiff, short puffs in the night air.

"We're almost there," George said. "You can make it."

"No," said Zuke.

"Then we'll leave you here. We'll get you on the way back."

"No," said Zuke. "Not with that coyote out there."

"Horse can stay with you," George said. "No coyote would mess with Horse."

His eyes looked to mine. *Right?* they said. *You agree, don't you?* And I didn't want to tell him no, that I felt the same as Zuke.

Horse still said nothing.

"No," Zuke told George again. "We stick together."

The wind crept up, circled around us, leaving icy bits of dust on our faces and the smell of brittle sagebrush in our noses.

George looked in the direction of the canal, toward the pomegranate trees, toward the shack where the Indian lived. And I knew he was thinking that Ralph Omura would be there tomorrow.

He sighed loud and kicked the dirt.

"Why didn't you watch where you were going?" he finally said to Zuke.

I FINALLY FOUND an envelope. I searched through Gila River like finding that envelope would bring Papa back to us.

I put Kimi's note inside, licked the sticky part twice to be safe, and wrote Mr. Bobkin's address on the outside as neat as I could, then bought a stamp at the recreation barrack.

I dropped it into the mailbox and looked through the barbed wire, west, toward California.

And I hoped he'd get that letter in time to feed Lefty.

MAMA GOT A letter from Papa. It was an actual letter from Papa. The first word from Papa.

"He didn't write it," she told us. "But I can tell they're his words. Someone must've written what he said."

"What does he say?" Kimi asked.

Mama smiled. She held the letter to her chest. She didn't need to open it again. You could see by the look on her face that she'd already memorized each word.

"He says the government is sending many men back to their families," Mama told us. "It could be a while longer, but he hopes to see us soon."

"Can I fold the letter into a crane and hang it next to Mr. Bobkin's, above my bed?" asked Kimi.

Mama thought about this.

"Hang it over my bed," she finally told Kimi.

I watched Kimi fold a crane, and I wanted to write to Papa now that we had his address. I wanted to ask him if he'd packed already, and did I sell too much of our furniture. I wanted to ask him if he missed playing catch with me, and did he get stomachaches from the food in Fort Lincoln.

But I knew he couldn't read English, and I didn't want someone else knowing these things before I did.

ON NEW YEAR'S Day, 1943, *someone* ran the Japanese flag up the hill pole.

"It was probably a disloyal," George said. "There are some of those in our camp."

"I haven't seen any," I told him.

George shrugged. "There's one in my block. He mostly keeps to himself."

We stood around watching it in the wind. The sight of it waving white and red, loudly, openly, over Gila River caused joy, fury, stifled smiles, and balled-up fists in the people walking by.

JANUARY 30, 1943, they served salt-and-peppered mountain oysters for dinner in the mess hall, which Kimi wouldn't eat. I sat next to Mama for the occasion.

They said it was in honor of President Roosevelt's sixty-first birthday. The newspaper editor whom everyone knew stood up toward the end. He cleared his throat loud enough to get our attention.

Then he looked around, like he saw the thoughts of all of us and he'd carefully gathered them together for tonight. And he said, "We pray that all the people in the United States as well as the world can someday live with mutual love and respect for each other regardless of race, color, or creed.

"For without its fulfillment, we Japanese Americans will lose everything we thought decent in this world. Our hearts will be dull lead inside a duller body. We will no longer live. We will merely exist."

And then he looked out the window, toward the future he

wished for, and a few adults and even some older kids, they nodded, and some eyes went watery.

Mama moved close to me, and patted my shoulder in a way that said, *Please pray for this to come true, Tetsu, even if you won't come with us to church service.*

Spring 1943

KYO'S PAPA STARTED work on the baseball field. He said that he got permission from the camp administrators, and they put him in charge even.

"The season's coming up soon. We have a lot of work to do before it gets here," he told us.

Kyo's papa handed out shovels and picks, and pointed to the area outside block 28 that he thought should be cleared first.

I spent the first day pulling sagebrush with roots that must've been a hundred years old. My palms bled from deep scratches, throbbing with every yank. My knuckles split from unfriendly jagged thorns. My knees became embedded with bits of gravel that made their way through the material of my pants.

I didn't stop working for lunch when everyone else did. I didn't want food. I only wanted to swing the bat over home plate and watch the ball take off between short and third.

I SAW GEORGE and Horse by block 67 after school one day. George asked why my hands were so banged up.

"We're making a baseball field behind block 28," I told him.

"Is that right?" he said. "Are you working on it with those two brothers who played baseball together? The ones whose father is a coach?"

"Yeah," I said. "You wanna help? We still got lots of sagebrush to clear."

"Naw," he said. "But Zuke might. He played center field for his team last year. Remember?"

Horse didn't say anything.

George smiled to a group of young girls climbing through the fence, tried hiding his broken tooth.

"Hi, George!" one of them yelled. "It's Akiko. We're going to see the pomegranates."

George smiled even bigger, then winked at the oldest girl.

After they'd walked far enough into the desert, I said,

"Everyone goes through here now. It seems like the rules have been forgotten."

George nodded. "Like I said before, no one cares if we leave. There's nowhere to go out here." He ran his hand through his wild hair, then spat. "You hear about the War Relocation Authority announcement?" he asked me.

I shook my head.

"They said second-generation Japanese born in America, the Nisei, are now eligible for the *army*. You *believe* that? They say as long as you're loyal to America, and answered *yes* to both questions on the loyalty questionnaire, you got the right to serve. They'll even train you in combat procedures."

"No kidding?" I said. "You're a loyal American, aren't you?"

George smiled. "Sure I am," he said. "But if I was old enough, I'd have answered yes just to get out of here."

EVERY DAY, KYO, Ben, and I would clear sagebrush and mesquite along the infield where Kyo's dad told us to, before school and after school.

We'd tell each other:

> *This is where first will go. Here's where second will be.*

And when the sun was rising up after breakfast, and the smell of summer blew in strong, sometimes I'd see my old team. They were running to take their places on the field.

I'd see Harold in right field and Marty Burns at short. I'd see my coach carrying a bucket of baseballs, and he'd be whistling some kind of happy song.

But then the dust would start up and I'd come back to Gila River.

There were adults who stayed during the day to help clear the infield while we went to school.

Each morning, as I walked off the field, I left the only part of Gila River I liked.

KIMI CAUGHT A baby king snake. She put it in its own box. And she told Mama—she was as serious as she could be— she said, "I'll keep him outside. He won't be allowed in. I promise."

Mama shook her head right away.

"But he already has a name," Kimi told her. "Kingie."

"It has to go," Mama huffed.

"Please," said Kimi.

"It's not poisonous," I told Mama.

"Plus, my lizards need a friend," said Kimi.

"I don't care," Mama said, and she looked past us both. "Put it back in the desert now."

ACCORDING TO MAMA, enough of the mothers at Gila River have complained about the ladies' latrine that they're thinking, finally, of installing dividers for privacy.

Mama tucked Kimi in bed, grinning, while a good feeling floated off her, like someone reporting they've just hit their first grand slam clear over center.

ONE MARCH MORNING, already feeling like summer, I cleared the outfield, tugging on a dried spindly bush, one I could tell didn't want to be pulled by the way it held so tight to the dirt.

I was talking to Zuke, who'd been coming to help out and reciting *every* catch he'd *ever* made in center field since he was seven, and you should've seen the time he dove for it and broke his wrist, when suddenly, I heard a sizzling buzz.

It started out low, then quickly grew loud enough to make me step back. That's when I saw it: a rattler, in the center of the brittle stick branches.

"Don't move!" yelled Zuke. "It'll sense your movement!"

The snake coiled and swerved. Its head reared up slightly, waiting to see what I'd do.

I stood as still as I could, like Zuke had told me. I tried not to breathe. I tried not to panic. I hoped my leather boots were thick enough to keep that snake's teeth from piercing through.

Kyo's papa crept up so quiet and slow that I didn't see him

coming until his rusty metal shovel slammed down on that rattler's head.

Instantly, the head dropped off, falling near the snake hole I hadn't seen. Its skinny black tongue went limp. Its scales glittered in the sun like they were wet. Its tail took its time, though; slowly, very slowly, it tipped to the side until finally it lay motionless on the gravel.

Kyo's papa gripped the shovel high above his shoulders, and you could see he was ready for more rattlers if he had to be.

Then he scooped up the body of the snake with his shovel and tossed it five feet in the distance.

I let out the breath I must've been holding, and fell back, tripping over a flat gray rock.

"You wanna keep the end of the tail, Tetsu—the rattle?" Kyo's papa said. "I can cut it off for you. That one's pretty long."

Zuke slowly stepped toward us. "You should keep it," he told me. "I would."

I leaned my body toward the dead snake, and looked over the clearish, waxy part of the tail.

It reminded me of Mama's string of yellowed pearls she'd tucked away in her bedding so no one would find them.

"Yeah," I told them as I stood up. "Cut it off."

WHEN KIMI SAW the rattle that evening, she sat up from her cot where she'd been resting with her cardboard box of lizards next to her.

She took the rattle from my palm and rubbed it between her fingers.

"Where'd you get this?" she asked.

"We had to kill it. It would've bit me."

Tears came to her eyes.

"It would've *bit* me, Kimi," I told her again.

"I know," she finally said. "But please, don't keep the rattle here. It reminds me of Lefty's bad eye that Mr. Bobkin wrote about. It makes me think he needs us."

So I took that rattle out of her hand and tucked the sheet around her. And then I walked out the door and buried it under the barrack. And I said this to her as I was digging that hole: "Don't worry, Kimi. It's gone."

AFTER ALL THE sagebrush outside block 28 had been pulled, Kyo's papa stood looking it over one night, his jacket buttoned tight around his neck.

It didn't look like a real ball field yet, but you could see the infield if you imagined hard enough:

Green grass,
chalk lines,
a white ball rolling toward third after a surprise bunt.

"We need to get all those rocks out of that dirt," Kyo's papa told us. "Otherwise, the ball will bounce up into someone's face if it hits the ground just right."

Kyo nodded and pulled his Yankees cap down tight.

"Tomorrow we start removing every stone bigger than a marble," Kyo's papa said.

I looked toward the desert. The night breeze blew in the smell of dust and gravel.

There must've been ten thousand stones out there waiting for us to haul them away.

It didn't matter.

I would've picked them all up myself if he'd asked me to.

MAMA WANTED TO order new shoes for me and Kimi from the Sears, Roebuck Catalogue. But they cost more than a person who makes sixteen dollars a month can afford.

"I can just push a piece of cardboard inside my shoe to cover the hole," I told Mama. "That's what Papa would do."

Mama frowned. I couldn't tell if she was madder about the cost of shoes or the piece of cardboard in my hand. So I said, "I saw a man by the recreation barrack last week who repairs shoes."

"I bet he has a lot of business," she told me.

"I'll go see him," I said. "Save your money for something Kimi needs."

KYO'S PAPA BROUGHT a bat to the field one night. He picked up small rocks from the pile of cleared-away stones, then threw them one by one into the air like they were baseballs, hitting them as far as he could.

Kyo, Ben, and I, we started running after them.

We fielded those rocks like we were playing a World Series game, and we didn't care how many times we crashed into each other, or how dirty we got, or even about skinned elbows.

We didn't care about the mess hall closing for dinner or torn pants, or the hole in my shoe getting bigger.

We just wanted to make the greatest catches ever in the whole history of baseball. And that night, each of us did.

KIMI'S PRACTICALLY GOT a zoo going. Three lizards, one quail, and four brown spiders, the kind that aren't poisonous with the long legs.

She lets the other kids pat the lizards. She brags about how the quail coos every morning, and how the spiders spin webs inside their cardboard box.

The day she turned nine, she set a pretend table of tea and cookies and gave each of her pets a small gray pebble hat and a dried-leaf lace handkerchief to celebrate.

When Mama told Kimi she had enough pets for now, Kimi said, "But they were *lost*. And someone had to feed them."

GEORGE CAME RUNNING to find me while I was clearing stones from the ball field.

"Tetsu! *Tetsu!*" he yelled through the fence.

I stood up and held my hand over my eyes, blocking the sunlight, to see him better.

He motioned me over.

So I dropped the wire screen I'd been using to sift out the smaller rocks, and ran to where he stood. I could tell something was wrong by the way he dragged a busted stick across the barbed wire.

"Remember the girls who went through the fence last week? The ones we saw that night?" George asked me.

I nodded. "Yeah, I remember."

He shifted back and forth, looked like he'd been up all night.

"The youngest one, Akiko, you remember her? She fell into the canal. A fisherman saw her. He tried to get her out. It took a while, and he finally rescued her. But she almost drowned. And now, she's real sick. They're making her stay in bed. No one is allowed to see her," George said.

He pushed his upper lip over his half tooth and shook his head.

"Those girls were trying to get the pomegranates I told them about," he said.

I reached my fingers through the fence and gripped the sleeve of George's wrinkled shirt.

He put his hands over his face. "She's only seven years old," he said.

The rest of the day, I sat next to my friend in the dust. And I never did find the words that came after *she'll be okay*.

THE NEWSPAPER RAN an article: SEVEN-YEAR-OLD RESCUED BY FISHERMAN.

And in between the words of the story, and the talk around camp, I knew George felt he was to blame. I knew it by the way he told Ralph Omura that he didn't care about those pomegranates after all. And he wasn't going back to that canal for a long time, maybe never.

EARLY ONE MORNING, when the roadrunners were still out, I was clearing stones from center field, and placing them in long rows along the first baseline to keep the dust down, because this was where the spectators would stand. This was where Papa would stand when he finally got here. Kyo's papa found me.

"Thank you for all of your help with the field," he said.

"I'm happy to do it, Mr. Tanaka."

"Tetsu," he said, "why don't you call me Coach Tanaka?"

I looked up at him. Sunlight streamed around his shoulders, making him look much taller than he was.

"Thank you, Coach Tanaka," I told him.

He smiled and walked toward where home plate soon would be. I watched the dust rise up from his shoes, then settle back down. I knew soon there'd be players running around the baseline, kicking up the dust even more.

AT SCHOOL, OUR teacher told us she had finally received some extra paper. It was enough so she could show us how to write business letters, and we could mail them off even.

"Think about the person to whom you want to write," she told us. "Don't forget to include all the parts of the letter: the date, the greeting, the body, the closing."

Kyo, who only took his Yankees cap off in school and the mess hall, raised his hand and asked, "Can I write to Joe DiMaggio's drill sergeant in protest? He got drafted into the army last week."

And the teacher nodded, and she passed out that paper real slow, and you could see she was sad to have it leave so soon.

"Try not to make any mistakes," she said as she gave us each one piece. "We may not get more for a while."

THE FIRST LADY, Eleanor Roosevelt, came to visit Gila River in April 1943.

Said she wanted to see for herself the conditions here.

She spent all day touring Gila River, and talking to residents, walking through barracks.

I saw her. She was twice the size of Mama, tall enough that she didn't need those high heels.

When she left, she told the newspaper reporters that the residents at Gila River were not being pampered like Americans had thought, and that she would not choose this situation as a way of life.

She looked pretty nice, but she didn't notice me or George standing there as she left.

"You hear about Admiral Yamamoto, the commander in chief of the Japanese Combined Fleet?" George asked me.

I shook my head.

"He was shot down by American P-38s. It's a real victory for our country since he was involved with the bombing of Pearl Harbor."

"No kidding?" I said.

"The guy was out on an inspection tour. He probably never expected to be killed."

I leaned up against the barrack, thinking how we surprised him the same as he surprised us when the Japanese bombed Pearl Harbor.

Summer 1943

KYO TOLD ME that his papa had been making secret middle-of-the-night trips to the lumberyard in camp.

"The lumber he takes is supposed to be used for things residents need, like building new structures," he explained. "The guards are Japanese, so they turn their backs when he goes there late at night. But still, he doesn't want to draw attention to all that wood, so he buys some, too. And then he buries a lot of it way out in the desert so no one finds it."

Kyo looked toward the horizon, toward far-off, sloping mounds of fresh dirt.

"When he needs it for the baseball field, he'll go and dig it out," he said.

"What's he gonna do with all of it?" I asked him, and I imagined some benches, or a batting cage.

Kyo glanced around, pulling his Yankees cap close to his eyes. He waited till two men walked past so they wouldn't hear. He could hardly stand still as those two men walked like they had nowhere to be.

Then he leaned closer to me and smiled. "He's gonna make a backstop frame," he told me.

I GOT TO pour the flour Coach Tanaka had squirreled from the mess hall to make the baseline from third to home.

I followed the string Coach set in place so carefully that it took almost an hour to finish.

Kyo and Ben yelled to me from home plate, "Hurry it up! What's taking so long? We wanna test out the field!"

"Tomorrow," Coach told them. "After school, I'll have the bases in place. Tell your friends to come to the first official practice."

GEORGE FOUND ME after school the next day. Horse was with him.

"Where've you been?" I asked George.

"Nowhere." He spat in the dirt.

"How's that little girl, Akiko, doing?"

"She's out of bed just today," he said. "I saw her walking to the mess hall with her mother. Me, Zuke, and Horse are gonna dig up those two giant saguaros today. The ones on the way to the canal with the three arms. We're thinking of bringing them inside the fence and planting them by her barrack. Other people have planted things from the desert."

George looked at Horse, and Horse didn't say yes, he'd seen saguaros being transplanted, too, but I'd gotten used to him not talking by then, so it was okay.

"Wanna come help us?" he asked me.

I thought of the ball field waiting to be tested out. "I'm glad she's doing better," I told him. "Our first official practice is today. But I'll help you after that."

George nodded, and he and Horse left to get Zuke, and you could see by how they walked away that they were on their way to do something important, equal to plowing a two-hundred-acre farm field.

WHEN I GOT to our barrack, Kimi had to go to the latrine.

"You have to take me," she said.

"You can go by yourself," I told her. I found my baseball glove and slipped it on, and I was one foot out the door.

"Mama said when she's at work, *you* have to."

"I'm busy today. You're old enough to go by yourself," I said, and in my voice I told her I had somewhere to be.

Kimi frowned. She blinked back tears, looking more tired than usual.

"Fine," I said. "You have to hurry, though."

She nodded quickly and we made our way to the ladies' latrine.

I saw Kyo and his brother, Ben, out in center field as I walked by. Ben threw the ball to his brother with a look on his face that made me want to get out there even more.

Hurry, I thought. *Hurry. Hurry.*

When we got to the door of the ladies' latrine, Kimi said, "Where's the pillowcase?"

"I forgot it," I told her, and right away, her face went stiff.

"You're supposed to bring it. Mama said so."

"I'm sorry. I didn't bring it."

"But I *need* it."

I glanced toward the baseball field. "Look," I told her. "Just try without the pillowcase today."

"I need it," she said.

She stomped her foot and sent dust hovering around her ankles.

"Kimi, I told you before, I'm busy today."

"Go get it, Tetsu!"

I crossed my arms. "No," I said.

We glared at each other, and I couldn't tell who was angrier. I felt the minutes wasting away, and decided it was me who was angrier.

I heard myself say, "Fine. If you don't wanna go inside, then I'm leaving."

And I turned, just like that, and walked toward the field, punching my glove, hard.

"Then I'm sneaking out in the desert! Like you, Tetsu!" Kimi yelled after me.

"Fine!" I yelled back.

I punched my glove three more times. I knew she wouldn't go into the desert alone, because she wouldn't even walk to the latrine by herself.

ON THE BASEBALL field, I formed the tip of a triangle, with Kyo and Ben each at a point.

Ben threw to me, and I threw to Kyo, and Kyo threw to Ben. I could feel that this field was going to be better than I ever imagined it would.

After a few minutes of warming up, we assumed our positions.

Me: first.

Kyo: catcher.

Ben: third.

Zuke came later and took center field, and the ball soared high white arcs between us.

Other players came, filling in the open spots, second and left and everything else, to form *one team*. It was like Christmas morning had come in April, and everyone got a new bike, and pancakes were cooking, and outside it was snowing. It was a feeling like that.

Later, when the small black bats darted between branches of yucca behind us, and the sun spread its last blaze over the desert, Coach Tanaka set down his bat and walked out to the mound.

He stood with his hands on his hips, squinting into the dusk.

I kept the ball in my mitt, waiting to see what he'd say.

Zuke ran in from center with the others. Kyo and Ben squatted down. It felt like there was nothing else in the world but us and the dirt field.

"We're going to have an excellent season this year," Coach told us. "You boys look pretty good."

His words were all I heard in my mind as I walked toward my barrack, forcing my feet to stay on the ground.

BUT AS I neared 28-12-B, Mama's eyes found me from the front door where she stood.

They took the weightlessness out of my feet and the smile off my lips. They stopped me from breathing in.

I dropped my mitt and ran to her. She grasped my hands in hers.

"Kimi is gone," she said. "Her lizards are gone. Tetsu, Mr. Bobkin's letter is the only thing that's left. I have looked everywhere for her. No one has seen her."

Her eyes searched mine, and I could see they were telling me the part she couldn't say aloud: how she'd given away everything she treasured, a lifetime of things, and she didn't know when my father was coming back, and she couldn't take losing one more thing.

And suddenly, I could not look Mama in the face.

I could not feel my hands clutching hers.

I turned away from Mama's eyes, and I ran as fast as I could to the fence behind block 67, to the place Kimi knew to go because of me.

TWICE, I FELL, skinning the palms of my hands, ripping the knees of my pants. I could not get to block 67 fast enough.

I was overwhelmed with worry, anger, then worry again. I felt like I might throw up.

I knocked over an old man I didn't see.

"Watch it!" he yelled.

I could not compose myself enough to say *excuse me.* So I grabbed his arm hastily and pulled him up. I couldn't look him in the face, either.

When I got to block 67, all sorts of kids were standing around.

"Kimi!" I yelled. *"Kimi!"*

I ran from person to person, pushing apart shoulders from tight circles, searching for Kimi's face.

"Has anyone seen a little girl here today?" I yelled.

Blank faces turned toward me; one boy shook his head.

Finally, I crawled through the fence and stood facing the desert.

It looked *different*, and bigger than anything I'd seen, more dangerous than any place I'd been. Darkness was stealing the last light, and there wasn't even a small moon.

I wondered, as I looked at that desert, why it suddenly seemed I'd never been out there before.

I RAN IN the direction of the canal because it was the only place I could think to go.

My feet staggered miles over rocks and dried creosote and gravel. My eyes searched left, right, behind me, in front of me.

I looked for anything that might be Kimi, the shape of her shoulders, the black of her hair.

I ran as fast as I could until I smelled the filthy canal water.

When I got there, I felt defeat spreading wide across the desert floor, over every nocturnal animal coming out for food. I felt it find my weary feet and legs and make its way up my body, heavy and satisfied that it'd won.

And I dropped down in the dust and cried.

I SAT ALONGSIDE the edge of the canal, aware of the air growing cooler. I worried about Kimi being cold.

I tried to remember her standing angry in front of me, her telling me to go back for the pillowcase, but I could not see what she wore.

My mind rapidly brought up memories:

Batting with Papa on the farm.
Listening to Mama sing to Kimi.
Throwing the ball to Lefty.

Dried blood stretched over my right knee.

I didn't care how dirty the mud water in the canal was. I reached down, cupped my hands together, and brought it to my mouth.

When I saw something move to my right, without thinking, I stood up and yelled, "Kimi!"

My eyes strained in the darkness.

I walked in the direction of what I thought I saw, wanting to find Kimi more than anything I can ever remember wanting.

I walked in the direction of what I thought I saw, but there was nothing.

AFTER HOURS OF listening to the canal water churn as I walked its crumbling dirt edges, I ran back to Gila River.

I could not think about the little girl named Akiko anymore, and how she fell into the water.

I could not think about the fisherman who'd rescued her just in time, or what would've happened had he not been there to save her.

So I did something then, because there was nothing else left, because I had no Papa to fix things, because Mama was alone clinging to a folded crane letter.

I stopped running when I saw Gila River on the horizon, and knelt down in the desert as the sun came up. I said I was sorry a thousand times. I said, "Please, just let me find my sister." And I promised right then and there, I promised I'd take care of her for real if I ever got the chance again.

WHEN I CLIMBED through the fence outside block 67, it was just after breakfast. I knew I needed to go to Mama to tell her I hadn't found Kimi.

A small group of older boys stood inside. They eyed me as I crawled through.

"Where are you coming from?" one of them asked me.

I glanced at the dirt on my clothes and the rips in my pants and the blood on my knee.

But then I saw what he was holding.

Slowly, I walked toward him, inspecting the cardboard box he held, until I was absolutely sure of what it was.

"That's my sister's!" I yelled out. "Where'd you get that?!"

I seized the box of lizards from him and took three steps back.

He lunged forward and pulled at the box, and I could hear the lizards' claws inside sliding around, their bodies bumping against the edges.

"I found it!" he yelled back. His voice was louder than mine.

People turned to look. Three boys ran toward us.

"Where? Where'd you find it?!" I yelled.

"I found it!" he shouted back.

He grasped the middle of the box. I could feel he was stronger than I was.

"It's my sister's! It's not *yours*! Give it to me!" I yelled.

I clutched the edges of the box as if they were Kimi, and I was a fisherman rescuing her from the canal. And somehow, he sensed the madness in me, softened his grip, and *let go*.

"Where'd you find this?" I said, and I made sure I held that box as tight as I could, backing away as I said it.

He gave me a look like I was crazy. He didn't want any more to do with me.

"In a bush over there," he said, pointing north. Then he turned to his friends, who laughed.

George was beside me all of a sudden. Horse was with him.

"Tetsu," George said, like I was a small child and he was my father. "What's wrong?"

"These are Kimi's lizards," I said.

George opened the box and picked up one of the lizards. "Your sister keeps lizards?" he asked.

"I think my sister is lost in the desert. She's been gone since yesterday afternoon. These are hers. She took them with her when she left."

I took the lizard from his hand and placed it back in the box. I wanted everything in its place where it belonged.

"Did you dig up those saguaros yesterday?" I asked George.

"Yeah. Both of them." George looked at Horse. "We gotta get more guys to dig holes big enough to plant them. They're tied to plywood right now."

"Did you see a little girl anywhere out there? Did you see Kimi?"

George looked up, and I saw him think a minute.

"No," he finally said. "I'm sorry, Tetsu."

WE STOOD IN a circle while I clutched the box of lizards and told them about my fight with Kimi and how I was sure Kimi wouldn't leave the camp.

Horse listened and looked me in the eye. He'd never done that before. And he nodded to me. He was saying something with his nod, but I didn't know what. Then he turned and made his way through the fence into the desert.

"Hey, Horse!" George yelled after him. "Where are you going?"

Horse walked north with his huge shoulders, and his size-13 feet, and he didn't answer, of course.

He just kept on walking like he knew something.

I FINALLY LEFT George and ran as fast as I could with Kimi's box to see Mama.

But when I got there, I knocked softly on the door instead of barging in, because I didn't feel like I should be allowed inside.

Mama quickly answered and took the box from my hands.

The lady from next door quietly passed by me, touching my shoulder as she left.

"They're Kimi's lizards," I said to Mama, though I was sure she knew this.

"It's all my fault," I said, each word a flash of lightning tearing apart our sky.

TWO MEN FROM administration came to check if we'd heard any news about Kimi. Mama politely asked them to come in, with their briefcases and hats and important gray suits.

But she kept her focus on me. She let me tell what I'd done, where I'd been, and everything I knew about the desert outside the barbed wire.

The taller man wrote down everything I said, and I heard the scratch-scratching of his pointed pencil on paper.

I saw Mama look through me to the perils of the desert I'd left out on purpose.

I saw the two men in their gray suits leave quickly.

I saw myself go from thirteen to Papa's age, trudging miles again, searching for my sister.

Outside, the sun flooded afternoon light across Gila River and shouted, *Hurry.*

KYO AND BEN stopped me as I rounded the outside of our barrack.

"Hey, Tetsu," Kyo said. "Your mother came over twice. Have you found Kimi yet? We've all been looking for her."

He squinted into my eyes. "You okay?" he asked.

I shook my head. "My sister is still lost and I've got to find her."

"We'll search the camp for her again," he said.

"Thank you," I told him.

And I took off running toward block 67 before they could say more.

GEORGE WAS WAITING for me when I got back to block 67.

"Zuke remembers seeing a girl yesterday afternoon before he left for baseball practice. He's on his way here. He'll tell you himself," he said.

I was studying the sun, deciding if I should wait for him, when Zuke and four other boys turned the corner.

"Go ahead, tell him," George said to Zuke.

"I saw a girl out there. We were digging up the cactus. She watched us from the hill for a while. I waved to her, but she didn't wave back. So I kept digging. When I turned around again, she was gone." Zuke shrugged. "I'm sorry. I didn't know who she was."

"I've gotta find her," I told them.

"I'll go with you," said George.

"Me too," said Zuke.

The three of us crawled through the fence, and we started in the direction Horse had gone: north, where every rock looked the same, where every bush was an exact replica of one I'd just seen. The sun brought sweat to the backs of our necks and foreheads, beating down on us relentlessly, screaming, *Give up!*

ONCE, WHILE WE were walking, I looked over to George. I could tell he was making his face look hopeful for my sake, but I saw what was behind his eyes. I saw it, and I had to look away.

BY THE TIME we found Horse, the horizon had turned hazy purple.

A solitary hawk flew a high circle above him, calling loudly into the evening air.

"Horse!" I yelled, while we ran to catch up. "Have you seen anything?" I asked him, but by the look in his eyes, I wondered if he'd even heard me.

"Horse?" George said, as he reached to touch his shoulder. "You okay?"

The wind kicked up the dust, and above us, the hawk yelled out again, so loud, so piercing, that everyone looked up.

Except me. Instead, I saw the yucca tree in the distance, the only shade around. I saw the spiny branches casting a filtered, thin shadow of lines onto a small figure curled up tight.

I could not get to that tree fast enough. I knelt down in the gravel under the shade.

Kimi opened her eyes and looked at me, and for a moment,

I could see she didn't quite remember who I was. I could see what she'd been through, how she'd done her best to find that shade.

"Kimi," I said. "It's Tetsu. You're safe now."

Her eyes softened like she'd just remembered the words to a song she couldn't recall before, and she reached her arms up to me.

But then her head fell limp onto the desert floor while the hawk called out three more times.

IT WAS HORSE who picked up Kimi and ran with her toward camp. We ran beside him with our hearts racing, pointing the way back.

"She'll be okay," George told me. And each time he said it, his voice was louder, like he was trying to believe it, too.

Our feet twisted over jagged rocks and thorny bushes, trying not to fall.

"She needs a doctor," I told George.

"When we get to camp, we'll go straight to the infirmary," he said.

We kept on running and pointing. "Hurry," I said to Horse at least a thousand times.

HORSE KICKED OPEN the doors of the infirmary with his left foot when we got there. He ran into the ward with Kimi in his arms, her hands dragging through the air, and found a nurse who seemed to know who he was.

The nurse looked at Horse and then at the rest of us.

"This is my sister," I said. "She was lost in the desert overnight."

The nurse quickly checked Kimi's pulse and pulled back her eyelids and put her ear to Kimi's mouth, and we waited for her to tell us Kimi would be all right.

She called for a doctor.

She called for a bed.

"Please," she told me. "Go and get your parents right away."

"I don't want to leave her," I said.

She nodded and motioned for Horse to place Kimi on the stiff white-sheet bed, while I held Kimi's hand.

The doctor came and took over, and the nurse put her

hand on Horse's shoulder while the doctor listened to Kimi's chest.

And I knew by the way the nurse's hand tightened when Horse turned his back to her that she wouldn't ask Horse how he happened to be carrying my little sister into the infirmary.

MAMA AND I sat across from each other for two days in the infirmary, waiting for Kimi to wake up.

There were no words between us.

But there was plenty being said by our twisted hands, and our stiff shoulders, and our silence.

I CAN'T REMEMBER when, but George and Zuke came to see us. And Kyo and Ben, they brought us rice. And the newly married lady from next door brought crepe-paper flowers.

I can't remember when, but Coach Tanaka stood behind me, and his hands were on my shoulders, and he said everything would be fine.

I can't remember when, but Papa appeared one night very late. He faded away before he could tell me what to do.

Horse never left us. He sat next to me, and he didn't move. I saw him blink from time to time, but that was all.

IN THE INFIRMARY, I heard a nurse in her hushed voice say to a nearby family that Japanese Americans could not be buried in Gila River, anywhere.

Sacred Indian land was not meant for outsiders.

"You may cremate your grandfather," she told them softly, "and keep him safely in an urn."

THE DAY KIMI finally woke up, Mama breathed out so loud it sounded like she'd been holding her breath long enough to swim across the Pacific.

I felt relief and exhaustion, and like a little crying kid. I thought I should be acting like a man, and was disappointed in myself that I was not.

I said thank you a thousand times.

And then I told the desert and the sky and the hawks, I told them I would take care of my sister and my mama, like I promised.

I was grateful for the dust devil that came along suddenly, which made everyone else clear out, and gave me an excuse for swollen red eyes.

I MADE A fishpond outside our barrack for Kimi like I'd seen others do. I dug into the dirt and lined the bottom with scraps of wood and stones, the sharp silver ones. Then I poured gravel inside until it held water.

George came by. He ran his hand through his wild black hair.

"I know where to get a fish for cheap," he told me. "There's a few fishponds around where people sell them. They used to get carp out of the canal, but now they have fish of all colors like they did back home. They've started buying them when they get permits to go shopping in Phoenix."

I waited most of the afternoon, replacing the water and putting more stones along the edges, until George came back with a red-orange fish.

"What're you gonna name it?" he asked me as he emptied it into the pond, then gave me some lettuce to feed it.

I watched the fish swim a slow circle.

"That's up to Kimi," I said.

MAMA TOLD ME Kimi's fever was gone, and that she'd be coming back to our barrack in a few days.

But Kimi would need lots of rest like people with valley fever do.

"It could take months for her strength to come back," Mama said. "The fungus got into her lungs. It rose out of the dirt from the wind and the farming, which stirred it into the air.

"You should go back to school now, Tetsu. See your friends, eat something," Mama said.

And I could see her trying to point us back to normal.

"I will," I told her.

But I sat all day tending to Kimi's fish instead.

We didn't talk about Kimi's valley fever again, but it was there all the time.

COACH TANAKA POSTED a sign outside the recreation barrack. It was asking for the aid of residents in building the baseball bleachers.

Any scrap lumber could be dropped off in front of the recreation barrack, and he'd pick it up later.

I walked by the pile of wood one night. I was on my way to fill Kimi's fishpond with more water. But I picked up a small two-by-four from that pile, rough with splinters and jagged ends.

And for a minute, I saw those baseball bleachers already built. I saw Papa sitting behind first base, where he usually sat, and that pile of wood had a hold on me.

But then I looked again at that two-by-four and decided it was better to use it to line the side of the fishpond than as part of a seat for someone who just wanted to watch baseball.

"THE OFFICIAL OPENING of the 1943 baseball season at Gila River is tomorrow," Kyo told me.

I stuffed my hands in my pockets and nodded.

"You should be there for the inauguration of the field," he said. "You helped make it."

I'd been trying to avoid Kyo and Ben, because when I was with them, I saw myself telling Kimi, *Fine. I'm leaving.*

Kyo looked at me like he didn't recognize my face, and he was just trying to find the guy who could hit the ball hard enough to get on base most times.

But I thought about my sister coming back to our barrack. I thought about how Mama would fuss to make Kimi comfortable. How I wanted to show her the fishpond I'd made for her, how if it wasn't for me . . .

"I'll try," I told Kyo. But I wondered how I'd get myself to that field ever again.

KIMI RESTED QUIETLY in bed each day, clutching her box of lizards, while Mama walked a commotion around her, and I paced back and forth to the fishpond wearing a deep path in the dirt.

Fall 1943

KIMI GOT A letter from Mr. Bobkin. It was addressed to her. He wrote that he'd been leaving food out under the California oak, where he last saw that dog who looked a little like Lefty.

And every time he went back, he found the bowl empty.

He said he'll keep this up until he sees that dog again, not to worry.

And Kimi, she folded the letter carefully into a crane, and Mama hung it above her bed with a piece of string.

It swayed above her and caused her to sit up against a pillow the entire afternoon.

KYO CAME BY to drop off my mitt.

"I've been keeping it for you since that day," he said. "Did you hear? The Office of War Information has put a ban on mentioning the weather during radio broadcasts of baseball games so no information gets to enemy forces."

I shook my head. I hadn't heard that.

"Some of the other blocks have formed baseball teams now that we have a field. We played against the block 31 squad and won. I was catcher. Ben played third. Zuke was in center. We wished you would've been there."

I put on a face that showed I didn't care about not being there, and shrugged.

We sat outside the barrack in the afternoon sun while he recounted every inning, strikeout, double play, and error of that block 31 versus 28 game.

I listened as he fed me his recollection of the first Gila River baseball game, like it was a bowl of soup or a tablet of aspirin he hoped was strong enough to make me come around.

A DUST STORM blew through Gila River so loud and angry, so brown and gritty, that part of a barrack roof escaped into the wind.

Mama needed an extra sheet for the cracks around the window, so she tore Kimi's white pillowcase to shreds and quickly stuffed it into the gaps.

"Don't worry," she told Kimi as she rushed around her cot. "You won't need it anymore. They've finally put dividers up in the ladies' latrine."

And I could see in Kimi's eyes, she was picturing the latrine, with its toilets, and its new white walls, and maybe even a mat for her feet.

KYO BROUGHT ME the new baseball.

"It's the official new ball by A. G. Spalding," Kyo said. "The middle is made of cork and balata. They say it'll be more resilient."

He tossed it in the air, then placed it in my hand.

"Wanna try it out?" he said. "I bet you can hit it farther than I can."

We both knew that wasn't true, and I saw him searching for what to say next, anything to make me try out that ball.

I squeezed the stiff white leather and tight red laces. I pictured it soaring over right field, with its new core, and the workers at A. G. Spalding smiling.

But I gave it back to Kyo.

"Thanks anyway," I told him. "Maybe some other day."

KIMI ASKED ABOUT the fishpond I'd been tending.

So I told her, "The fish swims all day in circles. His red-orange scales are shiny. The water ripples when you glide your finger across the top."

"I wanna take care of the fish from now on," she said.

"You will soon. You'll need to replace the water every day," I told her.

"I can do that."

"You'll need to find more stones for the bottom, and layer them up if the water level goes down too much."

"Okay," said Kimi.

"You'll have to feed the fish bits of lettuce. But not too much, or the water gets dirty," I said.

Kimi sat up in her cot and leaned toward me. She seemed all grown up just then, like she'd passed nine, ten, eleven, and twelve, and gone straight to eighteen, and she looked into my eyes.

"I know you love me, Tetsu," she said.

KYO, BEN, AND Zuke went to baseball practice every afternoon without me. They ran to the ball field like they couldn't wait to get there.

I watched them practice. Ralph Omura, who'd gotten the pomegranates before George, took first base in my absence. He was a lefty. I figured he'd be better than I was because of it, and decided to stuff my mitt beneath the barrack.

Ralph yelled to Kyo as they warmed up, "My father came back on the bus from Fort Lincoln yesterday. A few of the other fathers came back, too. I think that's almost all of them now."

He caught the ball, then threw it to second like he was making a double play. On first, and with a father who'd come back, he had everything I wanted just then.

Winter 1943

THEY OPENED A military truck motor pool in Gila River, along with a camouflage net factory.

"The administration has built a loading warehouse for all the supplies shipped by train for us," George said. "Only the warehouse is in Serape, eleven miles from here. Somebody's gotta get the supplies to Gila River by truck."

George knew everything that happened. I didn't know how he knew, but he did.

"You think they're gonna let you drive one of those army trucks?" I said.

George spat in the dirt. "Naw," he said. "But I can help them load it up in Serape. I can help them stack those supplies back here in Gila. Horse and I are going over to see about jobs after school. At least it gets us *out of camp*."

"Maybe I'll come," I said, because I wanted to get out, too. "When are you going?"

"Tomorrow," George told me.

GEORGE, HORSE, AND I got after-school jobs at the motor pool. It was because they needed lots of help. We rode in army transport trucks under faded green canvas. We filled supply orders for evacuees and stacked piles, and we filled thirty-gallon metal trash cans with blocks of ice, raw meat, skinned chickens, and rice, cramming the lids on tight to keep the flies out, then delivered them to all the mess halls in each block.

It paid twelve dollars a month and got us out of Gila River for part of the day, which we agreed was worth more than twelve dollars.

"They've finished building the sumo ring in block 29," George told me one day on our ride back to camp. "My little brother Zuke's been winning like crazy."

"Maybe I'll come watch," I said.

"You ever wrestled before?" he asked me.

"Once. But I was better at baseball."

"I can see that about you," he answered.

I turned away and peered out the back of the truck to keep my mind off baseball. Outside, things looked the same: 100-degree sun-scorched gravel, forests of saguaro, cloudless flat skies.

Each night, when I came back to my barrack and got into bed, I heard the news from Mama about more fathers who were coming back daily to their families. Just not ours.

THE CANAL INTERNMENT Camp baseball team got permission from administration to come three miles west to our camp and play a game on our field.

Coach Tanaka posted the news outside the recreation barrack, along with the day and time of the game. He placed an empty coffee can for spectator donations near the third-base entrance on the field. He was saving up for team uniforms.

He painted seat numbers on benches and erected a cover made of mesquite branches for shade for spectators.

When he saw me skulking around the edge of the field one night, he said, "I found a glove that looks like yours, Tetsu. It was under the barrack."

I shot him a look that said, *I don't know what you mean.*

Coach Tanaka nodded and looked up at the moon. It was shining a silver line from center through second to home.

"I'll keep it until you're ready to wear it again," he told that moon.

Spring 1944

KYO TOLD ME, "I thought you might want to know we're planting castor beans in the outfield. When they grow higher, they'll form a fence."

He pointed toward center field, then looked at me to see if I was listening. I was. I wanted to know about the new outfield fence, and he saw this, so he went on.

"If the batter hits the ball *through* them, it'll be a double. But if he hits the ball *over* the beans, it's an official home run." He smiled and touched his Yankees cap for good luck like he always did. "I'm gonna set the record," he told me.

HORSE WAS ALWAYS the first to arrive at the motor pool after school. He'd wait by the barrack till he saw George and me coming, and follow us to the army transport truck. We'd be wrapped in gasoline fumes, enough to cause a headache some days.

Horse would look out at the trail of dust rising through the heat and the glare, behind the wheels of the truck. He'd watch George and me play hearts with a stack of bent cards, and it looked like he didn't care about anything.

One day, on our way back from the warehouse, when the heat was pressing down hard, and the dust devils were acting up early, I said, "Horse, you wanna play cards with us?"

Horse looked down at his shoes.

And I said, "You wanna stack the wood today?"

Horse didn't answer.

And I don't know why, but I wanted to know all of a sudden why he didn't talk. So I said, "You got *anything* to say, Horse?"

George turned and looked me in the face. *What are you doing?* his eyes said to mine.

And Horse, he got up from his spot and moved toward the front of the truck.

We bounced over a hefty rock on the road, and the driver yelled, *"Damn!"*

When we got back to Gila River, George and I unloaded rough-cut wood, hoses, screens, and bags of cement mix.

Horse steered clear of me.

Finally, after everything had been unloaded, I marched toward him. I looked him square in the eye.

"Horse," I said. "Why don't you talk?"

Horse shook his head and looked away.

"Did you hear me?" I said, stepping toward him. I was aware of his strength, but it didn't stop me, and my voice was on the edge of something I didn't recognize.

"Why won't you answer?" I said.

George ran toward us.

"I wanna know!" I yelled at Horse. "I just wanna know!"

And then I pushed Horse's broad strong shoulders as hard as I could.

"What are you doing?" yelled George.

I stepped forward to let him know I meant it. I was mad about much more than him not talking, so I pushed him again and put my fists up. I showed him I was ready to fight my friend.

"That's enough!" a man yelled from the distance.

I turned around at once to the familiar voice and squinted through the ruthless sun.

We watched as the man came toward us with his stern, thin face and bony arms in a threadbare shirt.

He quickened his step as he neared us.

It was his hands I recognized first, the way they clenched tight and hung at his legs. The way they grabbed my shoulders firmly, how they felt inside my own palm when he took my hand and gripped it tight.

"Papa," I said, and I didn't know what came after that, but tears came to my eyes.

"I came to find you, Tetsu. Your mother said you'd be here."

I looked into his face, which was older and tired, but I could still see him there. I tried hiding my tears. I tried to show him I was a man, and that I'd done my best without him. I did not embrace my papa like a little boy would, though I wanted to.

Instead, I shook his hand once more, and kept a tight hold of it for a long while.

Finally, I glanced at Horse and saw he was watching us.

"I'm sorry," I told him. He didn't answer, but it seemed like he heard me.

So I looked over to George instead.

"This is my papa," I said.

George walked over, and he shook my papa's hand and said, "Nice to meet you, sir." I kept trying to believe that I was introducing *my papa,* who had finally come back to us.

And just then, two cactus wrens flew by with the makings for a nest in their beaks, and the sunset shined orange, and the breeze blew in the smell of night, and it was everything I wanted.

THE FIRST DAY with Papa back, a lightness came over us.

We didn't bring up Kimi's valley fever, or our old house, or the farm, or the war.

Instead, we acted like a family who still had a dog, where the mama baked sweet cakes for church, and the papa played catch with his son after dinner, and the little girl cut paper dolls, and wasn't sick in bed. And a baseball going through the kitchen window was the most terrible thing that could ever happen.

IT TURNED OUT the new electric lights Papa had hung over our outhouse, back at home in California, were being turned on and off enough at night when we used it that *someone* could've thought Papa was sending signals in Morse code to enemy subs or planes.

"With my involvement in the community, they thought I might be transmitting messages to the Japanese through the use of that light tower," Papa said. "That's why they kept me so long for questioning."

"Do you know who could have reported you?" asked Mama

"No," said Papa.

Mama shook her head. "Well, you *do* know how to build things well," she told him, half of her enraged, half of her proud.

THE SECOND DAY with Papa back, the desert wind flung brown and red and gold dust against our barrack and crept through its cracks, reminding us of where we were.

When the dust devil ended, Papa made his way to the vegetable farm where he'd been assigned to work. He rolled up his shirtsleeves and told us he'd be back before dinner. And Mama took a second day off from work in the mess hall, like it was something she wouldn't be needing anymore.

Summer 1944

THE POSTON, ARIZONA, Japanese Internment Camp decided to send over their own team of baseball players. They got a permit to play a five-game series at Gila River. A *series*.

Kyo went around like the Yankees themselves were coming.

"We drafted the roster," he told me. "We're hoping you'll play first. Ralph Omura can do it, but he's not as good as you are. Ben thinks so, too."

I crossed my arms over my chest, and didn't say yes or no, a picture of Kimi huddled under the yucca tree in my mind. Decided I might start up like Horse, not talking about things too hard to say.

Finally, I said, "Ralph Omura will do fine." Just like that.

PAPA SPENT HIS nights building furniture from found scrap wood.

He said to Mama:

You want a dresser?
How about a kitchen table?
Here you are: four chairs.

He hammered until he couldn't stand upright anymore, like each piece he assembled could make up for him being gone.

Our barrack filled with quiet wooden apologies.

KIMI FELT STRONG enough to walk to the fishpond. Said her lizards needed some more dirt, and her fish needed to hear a song and have some lettuce, and she wanted to be the one to give it to him today. She had a name in mind, *Shiny*, but she wanted to meet him first to see if it fit.

Kimi had to stop to rest in the dirt on the way there, though.

But her walking to that fishpond looked pretty good. It made me think everything could be normal again.

"The sun and fresh air did you some good today," Mama said as she tucked Kimi in bed that night.

I sat out front and leaned against our barrack while she slept, and heard the yells from game five of the Poston series drift off the ball field. I hoped she'd be able to visit the fishpond again tomorrow.

IT WAS A while before Horse would look me in the eye again. I found a seat next to him on the back of the army transport truck on the way to Serape.

After ten of the eleven miles in silence, trying to come up with what to say, and watching the dust rise up behind the wheels of the truck, I finally turned toward him. "It's okay, Horse," I said. "You don't have to talk if you don't want to."

Horse nodded like he was telling me something, but I didn't know what exactly.

So I stood next to him in Serape in the middle of nowhere by a desert warehouse, and the sun beat down, and the dust blew, and the hawks yelled.

We loaded two-by-fours. Our hands worked together, passing wood planks and making piles, until all that stiffness between us came undone.

KYO COULDN'T WAIT to tell me that so far this season, he'd hit the most homers over the castor beans. Most of them were in left field, but there were some in center, too.

He shrugged as he told me, like it was no big deal. But his eyes said, *I told you I'd set the record, didn't I?*

I FOUND KIMI'S red-orange fish dead in the pond. I scooped it out and placed it in a bag and saw all that going back to normal slipping away.

I carried the dead fish to George. "You know where to get another one?" I asked him.

"Sure," he said, his broken tooth showing. "But you gotta bury that one proper first."

"Where am I gonna do that?" I said.

"They got a pet cemetery now," George told me.

Horse came with George and me to the pet cemetery. Turned out it was behind the baseball field and to the south a little.

When we got there I counted eight cement headstones tucked between mesquite trees and sagebrush.

We read them aloud: six fish, one Gila monster, and one *dog* named Chubby.

"How'd they get a dog in here?" I said to George.

He shrugged. "Don't know, but they did," he said, like he

wanted to meet the person who got a dog inside Gila River.

The three of us shoveled a small grave with our hands, then dumped the fish inside.

"We need some cement mix for the headstone," I said.

"Let's use sticks for now," George told me.

So we broke mesquite branches and pushed them upright in the dirt around the fish grave until a jagged stick wall stood united.

I remembered the day we gave Lefty away, how he kept running after our car, and Mr. Nestor kept yelling for him to come back.

The memory of Lefty trying to keep up with us pushed down around me, until finally I had to leave. George and Horse stood up with me, like maybe they'd had a dog once, too.

George brought me another fish that night after dinner.

It looked almost the same as the other, with one exception: it was white, instead of red-orange.

"This is all they had?" I said to George.

"Take it or leave it," he told me. "But I'd take it if I were you. Everyone wants a fish these days for their ponds."

Fall/Winter
1944

COACH TANAKA ASKED to meet with my papa after dinner at the remote table no one ever sat at in the mess hall.

I watched from my table, tried to hear their words.

I wrestled my napkin into a wrinkled mess while Papa leaned forward and listened, and Coach Tanaka spoke with serious eyes.

When they were done talking, Papa stood up first and shook Coach Tanaka's hand, then nodded, like he'd be seeing him again, soon.

That night, before I went to bed, after Kimi and Mama were asleep, and the neighbors were quiet, and the desert wind outside turned calm, I said to Papa, "What did Coach Tanaka want?"

Papa sat down on his cot. "Something you may not want to give, Tetsu," he said.

And right away, I knew what Coach wanted, but I heard myself ask, "What?"

And Papa, he lay back, and I heard him sigh like he was deciding something.

So I said, "What?" again, only louder.

"There's another Japanese internment camp in Wyoming. It's called Heart Mountain. The baseball coach there has extended an invitation for a team of Gila River boys to come play a series."

Papa waited and let me take this in.

"Coach Tanaka wants you to go with the team. He thinks you should play first," he told the ceiling.

I walked toward Papa. I stood over his cot.

"Papa," I said, and I shook my head no, and my eyes filled with tears. "It was my fault Kimi got lost."

Papa sat up and put his hand on my shoulder. "Never mind that, Tetsu," he said.

"But I was playing baseball that day," I whispered. "I should've been with her. She needed me."

Papa stood up next to me. I was almost as tall as he was, and I waited for him to tell me that he agreed I shouldn't go to Heart Mountain.

"I told the coach you have my permission to go," Papa said. Then he sat back down on his cot, and made me take it from there.

COACH TANAKA HELD a team meeting at the recreation barrack.

Papa said, "Let's go." He even left the turnip field early.

Coach Tanaka went over a list of what each player should bring to Heart Mountain.

"It'll be a two-day bus ride," he told us. "We'll sleep on the bus. We're not all traveling together. We'll have two groups of eight, plus chaperones. We don't want to attract unnecessary attention in case the authorities stop us. I'll get work permits for everyone. We'll say we're aiding the war effort, heading north to help in the fields with the potato and sugar beet harvests, if we're questioned. Since many evacuees have gone to work the sugar beet harvests, this explanation should be acceptable."

He looked around at his players. *You understand?* his eyes said to us.

"We'll play a few games against the Canal Camp here.

We'll ask for donations to fund our trip to Heart Mountain,"
he went on.

Then he paced the front of the room like he was ready to
get on that bus tonight.

Papa and I walked to our barrack after the meeting. Papa
walked slow enough to give me room to talk if I wanted.

He didn't ask if I was planning to go to Heart Mountain.
But next to me, his walking said, *While I sure wish you would,
I will respect what you decide.*

"PLEASE TAKE ME to the fishpond," Kimi told me.

She was at the door and wasn't gonna let me say no. I could see that right away.

It was too hot to wear a sweater, but I put one on her anyway. I walked her toward the pond as slowly as I could. I wanted to tell her about her red-orange fish not being there anymore, but I didn't want her to get upset.

I wanted to run ahead and find some red dirt to rub on the fish. I tried to think of a way to turn her around, but came up with nothing.

When we got to the pond, Kimi sat down in the dirt. She watched the new white fish swim circles, while the sun glittered off the top of the pond water.

She didn't ask where her red-orange fish was.

She just sat.

"I'm sorry, Kimi," I said. "I wanted to tell you that your red-orange fish died, but I didn't want you to be sad."

Kimi nodded and swallowed hard.

When dinnertime came, and the lines at the mess hall started, I said, "It's time for you to eat. Let me take you back now."

"Not yet," said Kimi. She reached her hand toward the white fish, saying hello and good-bye at the same time. I didn't force her to leave for dinner. Because if you had seen her eyes, you'd have let her skip dinner, even if it would make your mama angry.

PAPA BROUGHT ME to a Canal-versus-Butte baseball game. He wanted to support the fund-raising effort for the upcoming Heart Mountain trip.

We dropped two silver dimes in the rusted coffee can where donations were collected, then sat along the first-base line.

Kyo was catching, and Ben was at third, and Zuke was in center. It felt strange to be so close and not be at first with my mitt on.

At the top of the second, Ralph Omura fumbled a hard line drive, and the batter from the other team ran across the base in front of us.

Papa sighed. He said quietly to me, "I'm sure he did his best. But you wouldn't have made that error, Tetsu."

The rest of the game was like that, with Papa cataloging errors that, according to him, wouldn't have happened if I'd played.

I LEFT THE motor pool later than usual one day and went to the pet cemetery with a bucket of warm hose water and a small bag of cement mix. I was sure no one would mind if I took it because I was only gonna use a little to make a proper gravestone for Kimi's fish, then put it right back.

When I got there, though, I had to keep my stomach from knotting, because I found Kimi sitting next to Horse by the fish grave.

"You shouldn't be here," I said to her at once. "Let's get you back. You okay? You feel sick?"

I dropped the water bucket and cement mix and grabbed her arm.

Horse quickly stood up.

"I wanted to come!" Kimi yelled at me.

"How'd you even *know* to come?" I said.

Horse looked at the dirt. I could see right away he was avoiding my eyes.

"I was feeding the fish at the pond you made me," she

said. "I saw Horse walk by. I asked him if he knew where the *red* fish went."

I looked over to Horse and he said nothing, like usual.

"You remember Horse?" I said to Kimi. "You remember that night in the desert when he carried you to the infirmary?"

"Yes, I remember. And I remember him staying with you and Mama, too. He doesn't like to talk," she said, like maybe I didn't know this already.

She sat down slowly, like she was feeling tired, and I went to help her.

"But Horse did tell me something today," Kimi said.

I eyed my sister, figured all this up-and-around must've made her hear things. "Let's get you back right now," I told her, picking her up and walking away. "You need to rest."

Once, I looked over my shoulder at Horse. He was bent over, mixing up the cement I'd dropped.

WHEN I GOT Kimi to her cot, I laid her down.

"Thank you, Tetsu," she whispered.

I covered her body with a light blanket. I knew Mama and Papa would be back soon from work.

"Horse said to tell you that I would've gotten valley fever even if I wasn't out in the desert overnight. And he would know," Kimi said.

Half of me wanted to believe her, but the other half knew Horse didn't talk. So I tucked that blanket around her the best I could, under her legs and her shoulders.

"He told me his aunt works in the infirmary. She's a nurse. He said people who live in the desert get valley fever sometimes," she said.

"Horse *talked* to you today?" I said. I was touching her forehead by then.

Kimi turned her head to the side, and she didn't feel too hot. She was closing her eyes to go to sleep, but she said,

"Horse has his own way of saying things. If you listen close, you'll hear."

I walked to the pet cemetery that night. I wasn't hungry for dinner, and I wanted to see the gravestone Horse had made.

I ran my hand along the uneven cement block, saw where Horse had dropped a little of the mixture by the side of the grave, how it had hardened over a branch of sagebrush and a quartzite rock.

FISH, the gravestone said.

Horse had pressed twenty small gray pebbles into the cement. They had hardened in the shape of a permanent teardrop.

I LOOKED FOR Horse the next day. I looked for him at school and at work and behind block 67.

When I saw George hanging around the mess hall, I asked him, "You seen Horse?"

George shook his head.

"Has Horse ever said anything to you?" I asked him. *"Ever?"*

George shook his head again. "Never," he said.

"You know if he's got an aunt here who's a nurse?" I said.

George pushed his lips tight over his broken front tooth. He looked up to a black hawk a quarter mile high with its wings tipped toward the sun.

"I don't know who he lives with," George said. "I think he's in block 64. He usually just shows up."

I nodded and leaned against the barrack next to him.

"You heard of anyone else ever getting valley fever here?" I said. I said it like maybe I was just asking about what they were serving for dinner tonight.

"I know an old guy who has it," George said. "And my mother knows this lady. She's got it bad."

"How'd they get it?" I said. This was not a question. This was me waiting for him to say that people who lived in the desert got valley fever sometimes.

"I heard it's in the dust," George told me. "Some folks say it's been here forever. Sometimes it gets into people's lungs and makes them sick."

I nodded when he told me, like I understood the whole thing. Then I stuffed my hands deep in my pockets and watched a group of girls walk by. They were giggling about something. They walked by us, and one of them looked back at me over her shoulder. I didn't know who she was, but when she smiled at me, I smiled back at her.

Two days later, Kimi told us that she felt almost like her old self again and that she was stronger.

It made Mama set aside her broom, and who cares about the floor today.

It made Papa put down his hammer.

It made me ask Coach for my mitt back.

THE SILVER TRAILWAYS bus had worn, ripped seats and windows that wouldn't shut all the way. It looked like it'd been driven around the world and back, twice.

I sat near the back of the bus and watched pine trees go by from my window.

I felt life rush in and out of my lungs.

I saw how, outside, things mostly looked the same as they did before we got to Gila River; people were driving their cars and filling up with gas, and families were heading to roadside diners.

After most of the guys on our bus had fallen asleep, and the driver had turned down the radio, Zuke came to sit with me. "I'm glad you're coming with us, Tetsu," he said.

I nodded and said, "Has Horse ever talked to you?"

Zuke stared out the window at the quarter moon. It was shining bright over a cloud that looked like the rear tire of a farm tractor. A large delivery truck rushed by us, rattling the bus.

"No," Zuke finally said. "Horse never told me nothing."

HEART MOUNTAIN, WYOMING, was a Japanese internment camp contained by buffalo grass, the Shoshone River, barbed wire, nine watchtowers, and a mammoth limestone rock, eight thousand feet high, stuck in the ground like it'd fallen by mistake from heaven.

Coach told us that they named the land here after that piece of limestone, and that it'd been there forever, and always would be. The guards waved us through as our bus neared the gate.

Heart Mountain had a farm going. It was like Gila River's, with peas, beans, cabbage, carrots, potatoes.

Heart Mountain internees had the same look on their faces as folks in Gila River.

Heart Mountain had bigger barracks than Gila River. Big enough for the whole team to fit into one.

Heart Mountain had darker dirt than Gila River. Cattle-raising, working-ranch dirt.

GAME ONE OF our seven-game series was against the Zebra Ayes of Heart Mountain. Coach said they had a few different teams we'd be playing against, and this was who was on deck first. I couldn't eat any breakfast—I had enough energy to go three weeks without food.

There was quite a crowd who came to see us play. I counted eight people deep along the baselines.

We warmed up with Ben at third, Kyo behind the plate, Zuke in center, and me at first. It felt like someone was putting a piece of me back where it'd been missing.

When that first batter stepped into the box minutes later, he swung at the first pitch to come across the plate, hitting a hard grounder to third. Ben threw high and fast, like usual, to me. I was ready for it. And when that ball found my glove, and the runner was *out*, it reminded me: *I'm a first baseman.*

I remember now.

I

remember

now.

Coach Tanaka nodded to me like I was part of the team. The crowd was roaring, and all of a sudden, I was back in California, and peanuts were in the stands, and there were no barracks lining the field, no watchtowers, and each dugout had twenty bats to choose from.

My first time up to bat, I let two strikes go by, then hit it between short and third, hard enough to get on base. Kyo smiled.

In the bottom of the sixth, their pitcher fell apart. He walked enough guys that it looked like a parade.

What seemed like five minutes later, it was the bottom of the ninth. The score was tied, 5-5, with our runners on second and third, and two outs. I got up to bat again, stepped back for a pitch that was low and inside. On the next pitch, I hit a high fly ball past the center fielder, bringing both the runners in to break the tie. Gila River won that game, 7-5.

GAME TWO: AGAINST the Zebra Bees. It should've put Kyo in the Hall of Fame. He had a first-inning homer with two RBIs, giving us an early lead. Then he hit a fifth-inning triple, and was driven in by his brother to score.

And that Heart Mountain pitcher, he gave Kyo a scowl and an intentional walk when he saw him again at the top of the ninth.

Coach Tanaka clapped his hands. He said, "That's okay, we'll take the base."

So Kyo stole second and third, just to show that pitcher he would've made it around those bases anyway.

That Heart Mountain pitcher got so mad, he loaded the bases with walks after that, then let up easy hits to the next two batters. Their coach met him on the mound for a conference, and by the way he handed over the ball, I knew he was being replaced. He stomped off the field like he was never coming back, and it wasn't his fault he'd met up with Kyo, or that Gila River got another win, 11-2.

GAME THREE: IT was a collision course with Heart Mountain.

The Zebra Bees' pitcher still lacked control, hitting three batters that came to home plate by the second inning.

Then our right fielder couldn't find first when the ball came to him, threw the ball over my head, and let a runner take the base when we should've had him out.

Ben took a line drive to his left kneecap and had to sit out the top of the fourth.

I grounded out twice and made errors that Papa would've had to turn his head from.

At the top of the sixth, I *struck out*. But Kyo doubled, then Zuke laid down a bunt that took their first baseman off base. Then the first basemen overthrew it to home, allowing Kyo to score and tie it up, 7-7.

In the ninth inning, our first two batters grounded out, but then came a triple from Zuke, a double from me, and a new personal home-run record from Kyo, for three more runs and another win, 10-7.

WINNING STREAK. IT felt like being alive.

It felt like Papa throwing to me on the farm, and Kimi getting well, and Lefty finding Mr. Bobkin's food dish.

It finally felt.

GAME FOUR ENDED at the bottom of the second with no runs on either side. A dust storm blew in. It caused our pitcher to throw wide enough to hit a surprised spectator.

People rushed back to their barracks while the dust spread thick across Wyoming, screaming, *No baseball today!*

GAME FOUR, MAKEUP: A shutout, 0-6. It was the first in the series the Heart Mountain All-Stars won, by not making any errors in a flawless defensive effort.

The closest we got to scoring was in the top of the sixth, our runners on first and second with one away. Then Zuke slammed a grounder to their third baseman, who threw it to second for the double play.

The rest of the game was like that, our team demoralized by sloppy fielding, overthrown balls, and even a hard hit through our left fielder's legs that resulted in two more runs.

Those Heart Mountain All-Stars walked off the field like they'd planned it all along. Their heads were high, and they punched their mitts and smiled under their caps.

They walked off the field like it served us right for the last three wins, and this series wasn't over yet.

They were happy to invite us to sit with them at dinner afterward so we could hear their victorious play-by-play once more.

GAME FIVE: HEART Mountain brought back their Zebra Ayes team. They were mixed with some old-time adult baseball players who wanted to play for fun.

We had to duck under wild pitches while at bat. We ran for measly grounders in the field, then walked leisurely to catch easy pop flies.

Kyo even batted lefty for fun. And on our faces, it said, *We're playing against a bunch of girls!*

But Coach Tanaka shook his head, and said, "Give those Heart Mountain players the respect they're due. They've been playing a lot longer than you."

So we all forced serious faces after that. We made it seem like we were struggling to keep up, and we even let them have their runs to be nice.

Then those Zebra Ayes, they went and surprised us. They caught us goofing around too much, and pulled a one-run win, 4-5.

GAME SIX: ERRORS by Gila River looked to be fatal. The Heart Mountain Zebra Bees took advantage of each one, plus, they added four homers by the top of the ninth.

When we came off the field in between innings, Coach Tanaka called us over. He knelt in the Wyoming dust and picked up a smooth, flat rock. No rock like that would've been on his field in Gila River.

We huddled tight around him, wiping sweat from under our caps.

Coach looked around our circle. We were behind by seven by then.

"You boys remember all those rocks you picked out of the dirt back in Arizona?" he asked.

We nodded together, remembering.

Coach adjusted his cap and dropped the rock in the dirt, and looked at us some more.

"While we were clearing that field, I thought about the

games we'd play. I thought about the team we'd bring together."

He stood up then. I could see him take it all in: the dirt ball field and the barbed wire. The faces waiting to see what we'd do next, wanting to forget Heart Mountain for a while.

Coach Tanaka smiled, and the Wyoming sun caught his brown eyes. "I couldn't want a better team, men," he told us.

From the way he smiled, I knew it didn't matter that we were going to lose that game.

That smile made me want to show him who I could be for the next game.

GAME SEVEN: THE series was tied, 3-3.

It felt like we were a regular team, playing in a regular series.

In the top of the fifth, with their team up and no outs, and runners on first and second, the batter hit it right to me. So I touched first and threw to second, who tagged the runner for the double play. Then, their runner on third got a signal from his coach and tried to steal home. But Kyo, he caught that ball from our second baseman, trapping the runner between home and third. He chased him down to complete a triple play!

In the end, we held Heart Mountain scoreless till the last inning. Then we let them have one run, just to thank them for their hospitality. Final score: 7-1.

Gila River ended the series with four wins, and we left Wyoming knowing we could be the players Coach Tanaka envisioned.

THE ROAD BACK to Gila River was much shorter than the road to Heart Mountain. And the songs on the radio, they were all sad ones.

And the whole time, an empty glass soda bottle rolled up and down the aisle, depending on what hill we were on, and nobody ever bothered to pick it up.

Road back to Gila River.

IT TOOK AN entire evening of me telling stories before Mama and Papa and Kimi had heard enough about the Heart Mountain baseball series.

Mama and Papa held hands on the edge of the cot, listening like I'd been somewhere resembling the moon and back.

When I saw Mama take the broom to sweep our barrack the next afternoon, I said, "Mama, did I tell you about the easy pop fly this old-timer hit in Game Five?"

Mama smiled. She'd heard the story already, but she set the broom against the wall.

So I made that pop fly last as long as I could, to give her time away from the dust.

GEORGE TOLD ME, "Horse hasn't shown up for school or work lately. Not since you left for Heart Mountain."

We rode the army transport truck to Serape to load new ventilators.

"You looked for him?" I asked.

"It's like he's disappeared," George told me. "No one's seen him."

After dinner, George and I headed to block 67, but found nothing.

Next day, same thing: nothing.

I FOUND KIMI sitting by her fishpond after school. She had her box of lizards with her.

"Please save your energy," I told her. "Don't spend too much time out here if you're tired."

"But I'm always tired," she said.

I sat down next to her and scooped out bits of uneaten lettuce floating near the edge of the water.

"You're feeding the fish too much," I said.

"I don't want him to be without food. What if he's looking for some, and no one's put it out?"

I moved closer to Kimi. I put my arm around her shoulders and threw the bits of lettuce back in the water. And hoped Mr. Bobkin was keeping that dish full under his California oak.

KYO GAVE ME his Atley Donald baseball card to add to my collection. Said he wouldn't be needing it anymore now that Joe DiMaggio had been discharged from the Army Air Corps, now that Joe DiMaggio would be playing next season again for the Yankees.

Said Atley Donald was 4-F, and not acceptable for military service.

Wondered how he ever could've liked Atley Donald when Joe DiMaggio was still around.

He didn't care who won this year's World Series between the Cardinals and the Browns.

Too many of the good players had been drafted anyway.

And next year, now that Joe DiMaggio was back, the Yankees would make it all the way again.

ON MY WAY off the baseball field one evening, I caught sight of Kimi. She was stumbling over a large rock with a handful of weed flowers, and I could tell she was trying not to be seen.

But I ran to her as fast as I could.

"It's getting too late for you to be out," I said. "Does Mama know where you are?"

A flower fell from her hand, landing near an empty snake hole.

"These are for my fish," Kimi said, and she was explaining away so I wouldn't turn her around. "I want to lay them on his grave so he knows I loved him."

I eyed the late orange sun, and the rising moon, and the dust blowing against the mountainside.

"Maybe tomorrow," I said, taking her hand.

She pulled free and stomped her foot.

She wouldn't let me carry her to the pet cemetery, so I held her flowers instead.

When we got there, we saw bats in the bushes, and *Horse* hunched over the fish grave.

I knelt down in front of the gravestone, and I said, "People have been wondering where you've been, Horse."

Horse stared straight ahead like he was seeing something.

I said, "You wanna come back to camp with us?"

Horse tightened his jaw.

I said, "I can walk with you to your barrack."

And Horse, he stood up quick. He broke a long stick off a yucca tree, and scratched the word *STOP* in the gravel.

I couldn't believe he'd done it, practically *talked*. I had to look it over twice to be sure, but it was there in the dirt for anyone to read.

So I took a step toward him, and I was taking a chance on pushing too hard. I could see he didn't want any pushing. But I said, "Stop what?"

Horse clenched his mouth, and it looked like he was about to yell out something. But he bent over the gravel, and the dust blew his black hair to the side and caught in his eyelashes.

I stepped next to him, hoping he'd tell me.

Horse kicked a quartzite rock loose from under a bush, and you could see he was real angry now. He gripped the thorny stick and scratched, *Stop talking to me like you know me.*

And then he hurled that stick in the bush, and marched toward camp with dust rising off his shoes in little puffs.

I didn't go after Horse. Kimi wouldn't be able to keep up, and I knew Horse didn't want me to anyway.

I just let him be mad.

I SKIPPED WORK at the motor pool the next day and made my way to the infirmary.

I wasn't sick.

I wanted to find out if Horse had a nurse for an aunt. If Horse had anyone.

I stood outside that infirmary and watched for the nurse who'd taken Kimi in that night. I remembered her hand on Horse's shoulder, how she had gone stiff when Horse turned his back to her.

I waited through dinner outside that infirmary. I waited through baseball practice, and a twilight dust devil. I waited until I knew Mama would start to worry, but I saw no one who looked like the nurse that'd taken Kimi in that night.

WHEN THE CANAL Camp came back to play a baseball game against us the next day, Papa was the first in line to drop a dime in the coffee can. He was our biggest fan.

He found his usual place along the first baseline. He said he wanted to see some of what had gone on in Heart Mountain. Told the man sitting next to him how I'd made captain of the city league in California by age twelve.

And Papa, sitting there, on the first baseline squinting into the sun to see me play baseball, he looked like he'd never been to North Dakota for FBI questioning, and he'd never lost his farm crops or the lease on the land, and he would, at any minute, pull money out of his pocket for a new tractor somehow, and a new life, and everything would be fine.

I DID MY best catching at first—no errors, and two double plays at second. I did my best hitting—one double, and one hard grounder through the castor beans. I saw that same girl who had smiled at me. She was with her friends on the bench, giggling about something and looking at me.

In the top of the eighth, when we were one run behind, I stood over home plate at bat. I waited for a hanging curveball, my favorite. I let two strikes go by, hit one foul, then found what I wanted. The pitcher hung one up, and I drove the ball high and deep to right field, so high it went *over* the castor beans, like I was Kyo.

I ran those bases leisurely enough. I let Papa have time to tell everyone around him that I was his son, the one rounding the bases, the one who'd just hit it out of right field.

Coach Tanaka met me at home plate, waving a *five-dollar bill* in the air, and he stuffed it in my hand and smiled at me as big as Papa was.

"Nice hit, Tetsu," he told me. "Your first home run."

I looked over to Papa, and he was still telling the man next to him, pointing over right field, and his face looked like it used to.

GEORGE SAID HE knew where to find Horse. He said, "He's in the desert. I heard he went for *pomegranates*."

So we finished our work at the motor pool as fast as we could and made our way through the desert. I told George—for the third time—the words Horse had scratched in the cemetery dirt. I told him how he'd marched back to camp without us. I told him how I'd looked for the nurse but didn't see her.

When we got to the canal, we saw three boys swimming in the brown water, and Horse sitting along the side with a bag in his hands.

George and I sat down next to Horse. Our shoes were half the size of his. We pushed dirt clods into the water, and George said, "You been here long, Horse?"

Horse watched the boys who were swimming while a pair of lizards ran over his left hand.

The three boys splashed mud, and yelled for us to come in.

"Don't you know that water's contaminated?" George yelled back.

The boys splashed harder, sent mud flying like they didn't care about unclean water when there was heat like this.

George picked up a handful of dusty gravel and let it sift through his fingers. "You got pomegranates in that bag, Horse?" he said.

Horse stood up slow, then handed the crumpled brown bag to him like he'd planned it all along.

George opened the bag and peered inside. His eyes looked like Horse had given him a bag of gold coins. "We finally got some, didn't we?" he told Horse.

Then Horse, he started back for camp. He looked over his shoulder at us. *You coming?* his eyes said.

So George and I ran to catch up.

That was how it was gonna be. Horse's eyes doing all the talking again.

PAPA CARVED TWO birds out of scrap wood for Mama and Kimi for Christmas. We went to dinner at the mess hall, where they served ham. Papa said he would give me my gift when we got to our new home someday, and he could build me another batting cage.

It didn't matter about the gifts or the dinner. Being together was enough.

Spring 1945

PAPA WENT TO a meeting held by Dillon Myer, director of the War Relocation Authority.

California, Mr. Myer said, will treat Japanese Americans fairly as they move back home from the relocation centers.

Evacuees, he said, should think about leaving the camps, and return to normal life as much as possible.

The WRA, he said, will help with job placements and financial support to a certain extent.

Nineteen forty-five, he said, should be faced with new hope.

Papa told Mama this in a hushed voice with stiff, crossed arms, like he wasn't sure which part he should believe, since all this came as a surprise.

But he brought back proof from the *Gila News-Courier* the next night. He sat on his cot after dinner and pulled a crumpled scrap of newspaper from his pocket. I don't know how long it'd been there, but it looked like a while by how wrinkled it was.

"There's a four-hundred-acre vegetable farm that needs workers." He read aloud: "'Housing, equipment, water, all are available. Sharecrop or cash rental. Interested persons should write to the landowner.'"

But Mama didn't stop her sweeping. She didn't say, *Let's write to the landowner.*

So I saw Papa decide what to do. He left the newspaper scrap on the table so the words could sink in and make themselves at home inside Mama's thoughts.

I FOUND KIMI sitting next to her fishpond. Kimi was up and around most every day now, collecting fresh dirt and leaves for her lizards. Her cheeks looked fuller and her face had more color, and she was even going to school again sometimes.

I sat down with her and watched her white fish swim around the edge of the pond.

A dust devil swung by. It missed us by eight or ten feet, sent scraps of paper and bits of gravel swirling to the top of the pond.

We were holding our breath and covering our noses and mouths, waiting for it to pass, when Horse suddenly bent over Kimi and draped a handkerchief over her head.

He stood behind her until the dust turned the corner and made its way toward block 29.

Kimi looked up at Horse. "You wanna sit with us?" she asked him.

Horse folded the handkerchief, taking a long time, like the folding was helping him decide.

"You wanna feed my white fish today?" Kimi asked.

He sat down on the opposite side of the pond like that was his answer.

She took a piece of lettuce from her pocket and tore off a bit, then threw it into the water.

The fish gulped it quick and waited for another.

Kimi handed the lettuce to Horse. "I miss my red-orange fish today," she said.

Horse tore off a piece of lettuce and dropped it in the water.

I tried not to notice the tears in his eyes. I knew he wouldn't say what was wrong.

But Kimi stood up and walked over to Horse. She didn't care about giving him room with his tears. She told him, "He'll never be a red-orange fish. But he can be a white fish."

OUR NEIGHBORS DECIDED to leave Gila River and move to Ohio. They'd heard from other evacuees who said they'd even made friends in Ohio, and not just hello–good-bye friends, but real friends.

Their children are back in real schools, and some of the Japanese mothers have been named members of the local PTA.

"Many people have started to leave since Dillon Myer's meeting," she told Mama. "You should think about it, too. They're talking about shutting down the camp soon. The WRA will help you relocate if you need it."

Mama smiled at her plans, and later, when she thought no one was watching, I saw her run her fingers over the scrap of newspaper still lying on the table.

That night, before she went to sleep, when Kimi and I were in our cots, I heard her whisper to Papa to write to the farm owners.

The moon was shining silver through our window just then. Its light fell in a straight path across the floor, up and over our sheet wall, to Papa's hand patting Mama's.

PAPA HEARD THE announcement. President Roosevelt had died. He was only sixty-three.

Papa said the president was having his portrait sketched when he fainted, and he never came back around.

Papa said the U.S. government had already sworn in the vice president, Harry Truman, from Missouri. And that he would have to be briefed on the war so he could lead our armed forces.

Papa said that tomorrow, throughout Gila River, there'd be a fifteen-minute quiet period at nine o'clock, so we could show our respect.

AFTER A WEEK off from all practice, or any talk of baseball, while we'd been showing our respect, Coach Tanaka called a meeting.

"I've made some changes to the lineup," he told us. "The Canal Camp has challenged us to another game." He looked around the field at his players kneeling in the dirt, and I could tell he already saw us winning that game.

When he told us to take our positions, he sent me to the pitcher's mound.

I said, "Coach, I've always played first."

Coach Tanaka nodded. "I know," he said. "I've been watching you throw. Let's see what you got, Tetsu."

He crouched behind home, where Kyo usually was. He punched his catcher's mitt and pulled his mask over his face. I stood on that pitcher's mound, which didn't feel anything like first, and I saw seven faces turn suspicious, like they didn't think I could pitch.

The first five I threw were low and outside. I heard Ben throw his mitt in the dust behind me.

Coach Tanaka stood up. "Bring your leg up higher, Tetsu. Let go of the ball sooner."

So I threw it again, low, but straighter.

Coach Tanaka punched his mitt again, and he was just getting warmed up. He sent two fingers down. "This is for a fastball!" he said.

I wondered if he thought I had anything *but* a fastball. Ben was sitting on third base by then, and I could see that he didn't think this was a good idea when we had a game against Canal coming up.

But I threw it again anyway. I threw it into the strike zone *three times in a row.*

Coach Tanaka smiled. "I knew you had an arm there," he said. "Tomorrow, you can practice some more."

Ben was on his feet again, smiling like maybe he'd just found a buried Indian arrowhead.

After practice, I ran to my barrack as fast as I could so I could tell Papa he just might have to change where he usually sits for the next game.

PAPA TOOK THE news in, the part where I threw the ball into the strike zone three times in a row. And he walked to dinner with Mama that night like he'd just been named the new vice president to take Harry Truman's old place. He asked twice when the game against the high school team at Canal's camp would be, so he could be sure he got off work early that day.

Papa borrowed a bucket of baseballs and an old catcher's mitt from Coach Tanaka the next day.

"Practice makes perfect," he told me.

And he meant it. Every day after baseball practice was over, he knelt outside our barrack. He tried to be the best catcher he could, so I could be the best pitcher I could.

MR. BOBKIN SENT another letter to Kimi. This time, it didn't tell about his horse named Red. It didn't tell about his California oak. It didn't tell about the weather.

It had only three words:

See enclosed photograph.

Kimi took that enclosed photograph and held it out in front of her, her thumbs pressing over the edges real tight, like the picture might slip off if a breeze came through.

"What is it?" I asked her.

In a quiet voice, she said, "Look, Tetsu. It's a picture of Red."

She passed the picture to me so I could see for myself the picture of Mr. Bobkin's horse.

"And next to Red . . ." Kimi said, and she was nodding,

her eyes were shining, and she was standing up straight like she'd just grown a foot taller.

"Next to Red, it's Lefty," she said.

See enclosed photograph.

LEFTY LOOKED LIKE he'd gotten in some kind of fight. But it was him. He had one bad eye and needed a good brushing and a long bath, but he didn't care.

You could see by the way he sat tall next to Red, with his tail curled, that he'd done what he had to do to make it back home.

You could see that he'd be there, waiting for us to give him a good brushing and a long bath. And that he wasn't going anywhere.

WHEN MAMA AND Papa came back after work, Kimi showed them the photo. She'd been waiting out front for them because she couldn't wait inside anymore. She told them the news and pointed at Lefty, and yes, it was him, we were sure.

Papa gave Mama his newspaper, and he picked Kimi up high into the air. He was laughing by then. Mama was smiling like you'd never seen, while I was saying what a good boy Lefty was.

And there we were: a family who still had a dog.

I KNEW BY the way Coach Tanaka walked onto the field the afternoon of the Canal game that he wasn't going to put me at first.

He wanted to see some more of my fastballs come across home plate.

Papa sat in his new spot. He watched me warm up on the mound and lifted his fist in the air, thumbs up, and I saw myself throwing strikes.

It took me till the second inning to find my rhythm, but I did. I made those Canal players swing when they weren't even close to hitting the ball. And each time another batter struck out, I threw faster, and that dirt mound started to feel like a familiar chair I'd sat in my whole life. I even got up the nerve to wave to the girl who had smiled at me. She was in her same spot with her friends again, watching me.

Papa brought back the newspaper the next day and stood in the middle of our barrack. He read, "'Butte defeated Canal by a score of 14 to 3 yesterday.'"

And then he cleared his throat and stood up straighter.

"'Tetsu Kishi pitched a tight game, allowing only one run up to the fourth inning,'" he read.

Then he stuffed that newspaper in his back pocket and walked around the rest of the day with it there, in case he needed to read it to anyone else.

AT PRACTICE ONE day, Coach Tanaka told us, "No need to put your gloves on. We're just going to talk today."

So we circled around and waited.

Coach Tanaka looked around at us like he had something important to say.

"As you know, we haven't played any teams besides other internment camps, and there's a powerhouse team you boys haven't met yet," he told us. "They've been the Arizona State champs the last three years in a row. Their pitcher's set all kinds of records. He'll probably play pro ball someday."

He looked toward the mountains. I could see him wishing that maybe one of us would play pro ball, too, someday.

Then he turned back to us. "I've been in contact with their coach," he said. "I've let him know that we'd like to challenge their team."

We looked around at each other and smiled.

"The problem is," Coach said. "We can't play on their field. Not while this war is still going on."

I could tell there was something more he wanted to say, but he just shook his head.

"So," Coach finally said, breaking the long silence. "I've invited them here. To our field."

"What'd they say?" Kyo asked his papa, and you could see what he wanted the answer to be.

Coach smiled. He adjusted his cap and made us wait. "They'll be here in two weeks," he finally told us.

FROM THEN ON we practiced baseball before school, went to school, practiced baseball after school, ate dinner, then practiced baseball again till there was no more light.

Kyo said he slept with his mitt on.

But still, every time we gathered on our field, their Arizona State champion title grew bigger.

It blew through the dust and the castor beans. It made us strike out unexpectedly.

KYO TOLD ME his papa was making plans to go back to California.

"He's been offered a job as a youth baseball coach near where we used to live," he said. "He thinks he can get me and Ben on his team."

"That's good news," I told him. "When will you leave?"

"In about a month. He wants to stay through the game against the state champions."

I nodded and looked him over. "I'll bet you'll be the best hitter on the team, like you are here."

Kyo smiled. "Naw," he said. "But thanks."

PAPA HEARD BACK from the farm owners that he'd sent his letter to. They wrote that they'd already filled the field positions they needed, but thank you very much for inquiring.

Mama started sweeping.

Papa told her, "There's other farms in California that need workers."

Mama paused to look at him long enough to let him know she wanted him to start looking for those other farms in California right away.

KIMI TOOK HER lizards out to the edge of the pet cemetery. She had a photo of Lefty now to take their place. She said she'd been planning it for three days, and I had to be there with her. We walked to the edge of the pet cemetery, 113 degrees in the shade.

She lifted the lid off the cardboard box and shook out the gravel. We watched the lizards slide into the sunshine.

They lingered at first, their claws digging into the red and brown and gold dust, like they were remembering what to do in the Arizona sunshine in the middle of the desert.

Kimi took a stick—it was a straight one I'd broken off for her—and gently pushed their wrinkled bodies forward. She told them, "Go. It's time to make your way home."

The lizards scurried away, one under a nearby yucca, and the other to the top of a rock.

"You can do it," Kimi told them. "It's been done before."

PAPA FOUND A new ad in the newspaper—a 125-acre fruit farm in California, workers needed.

"It's just seasonal for now, only four months a year," he told Mama. "But it includes housing, electricity, and water. The wages are fair. And there's schools nearby."

Mama nodded and gave Papa all her attention.

"It's thirty-five miles south of our old house," he said.

Then she sat down on her cot. She was listening good.

"There's a poultry farm close," Papa said. "They say they'll share their eggs. You could get back to baking," he told Mama.

Mama smiled and looked out the window, and I could tell she was seeing rows of sweet cakes lining the counters, inside her very own kitchen, inside her very own house.

Papa didn't want to take any chances. He made arrangements to use the telephone so he could call that farm owner.

When he came back from administration to tell us he'd

been offered the job and could start anytime, Kimi found a piece of paper right away.

"I have to tell Mr. Bobkin we'll be there to get Lefty," she said.

"Make sure you thank him for feeding Lefty," I told her. "Make sure he knows we'll be there soon."

GILA RIVER WELCOMED the Arizona State baseball champs when they arrived in their yellow school bus.

Their coach drove slowly into our camp. He looked like he was shocked that we were living here.

They filed off their bus, then gave us a once-over and let us see what state champs looked like.

Outside block 28, coffee cans filled quickly with dimes, and the stands swelled with more spectators than ever before.

It seemed all of Gila River had become baseball fans.

PAPA USHERED MAMA and Kimi to his new spot behind home plate.

George sat behind first base and yelled out my name eight or ten times. Then he did the same for his little brother, Zuke.

I saw that same girl again with her friends. She was looking at me, and I started wondering what her name was.

Even our teacher who'd volunteered to come to Gila River was there.

But it was seeing Horse that made me stop while I was warming up on the mound.

I'd never seen him at the baseball field before. He walked in front of the nurse who'd taken Kimi in that night. It was her, I could tell right away.

And when he came to an open space behind third base, he sat down, and the nurse sat down next to him. She turned and talked to him, but she didn't wait for him to answer.

Then she glanced at me. It was by chance, but she looked right at me, and I held her eye long enough that she remembered me. I could tell by the way she turned back to Horse and whispered something to him.

Then the nurse stood up and fixed her right hand over her eyes to get a better look through the desert sun.

I dropped the ball in the dirt and walked toward her. The nurse made her way through the crowd to the edge of the third-base line.

We stood across from each other with the third-base chalk line in the dirt between us. And she took my hand in hers, like it was something she'd done many times before.

"How is your sister?" she said.

"She is much better," I told her. "Thank you."

"I am Horse's aunt, May. We were not properly introduced that night." She glanced back at Horse. "Thank you for being a friend to Horse," she said to me.

And I wondered how she knew. "Did he tell you that?" I asked. "Did he tell you I was his friend?"

She looked at the ground. "No," she said sadly. "He tells me nothing. He has not talked to anyone since his parents died in Pearl Harbor. His father was a fisherman. His parents were on their boat when the bombs were dropped."

She let go of my hand then, and looked at me like she knew the same part of Horse that I did. "I am his only family now," she said.

"I'm very sorry to hear of his loss," I said. "I never knew why he wouldn't talk."

She looked up to the sky. "I've learned that if I pay close attention to him, though, he is very clear about most things."

"I've seen that, too," I told her.

I could tell she was pleased that I understood.

"Today," she said, standing up straight again and smiling. "Today, Horse brought me here to your game. It is the only time he's brought me anywhere with him."

She looked back again to Horse, sitting behind third base, in a way that told him she would've gone anywhere he wanted, that any place would've been fine with her. Then she turned to me, as the state champs ran out from their dugout, and the crowd began to holler, and the umpire swept off home plate.

"And that is a start, at least," she said.

COACH TANAKA CALLED us off the field to our dugout then, as the state champs took their turn to warm up on the field.

"It is our privilege to play this team," Coach told us. "Out here, we are all ballplayers, equal in every way."

Minutes later, the umpire called for balls in, and the crowd hushed, and Papa stood up so he could watch me.

FROM THE VERY first inning, those state champs played like they all held records, like they'd all play pro ball someday. They scored four runs, while Gila River got nothing from their pitcher. I did not look at Papa on purpose.

In the bottom of the second, though, we came back with four runs to tie the score. Showed them we could keep up with a team of state champs. But then they scored one more in the fourth and three triples in the fifth, for a 9-4 lead. And when they came off the field, you could see it in their faces, thinking they'd already won.

It was Kyo who started it in the bottom of the sixth. He got a double, and that was enough to make us start believing in ourselves again.

Then Ben, he homered, and Zuke tripled, and we told those state champs we weren't gonna let them win just yet. Coach Tanaka tallied *five more runs* for Gila River by the bottom of the seventh for a tied score, 9-9.

Top of the eighth, they scored one more, but we came

right back when our right fielder tripled and was driven in by Ben, evening it up for a 10-10 tie.

The ninth inning came, and the crowd stood and yelled with fists waving. The state champs looked so surprised as they took their places that a team from the middle of the desert, on a made-from-scraps dirt field, could come up with enough runs to have a tied score going into the ninth.

Both teams showed a strong defense on the field with no runs, and the game went into extra innings after a scoreless ninth.

Those state champs never would've thought that they'd get nothing from me. Me, who'd let them get hits up until now.

First batter up, I threw a fastball to the outside corner, a strike. Then a curveball, which he backed away from, that went right into the center of the mitt—another strike. Then one ball, high and outside. Then another fastball, which that batter swung at and missed.

Next two batters, three strikes in a row. They left the top of the tenth whispering to each other and looking me over, explaining it to their coach.

Bottom of the tenth, and Zuke was leadoff. They sent him to first on four balls.

Then our shortstop got on first with a bunt, which moved Zuke to second. The crowd roared, and the sun blazed.

Me up next. I stepped into the batter's box and had to duck under a wild pitch. Then I waited through two fastballs, which were both strikes, until I saw a curveball. I hit it hard, straight to the first baseman. He scooped up the ball and touched the base before I could get there. But Zuke and our shortstop took second and third, and I saw Papa pat Mama's hand, *That's all right, two runners advanced.*

Ben up next, and I handed him my bat. *I'll bring them in,* his eyes said to mine. *Don't worry.*

Ben hit a low fly ball to third that was easily caught by a state champ third baseman.

Kyo came next in the batting order. He walked to home plate with a serious face, took his time getting there.

He was the only one of us who could've stood up to two outs in the bottom of the tenth against a team of state champs in extra innings.

He looked so sure standing over home plate. He waited so patiently through *three straight balls*, all high and inside, and I thought for sure it'd be an intentional walk.

He knew what he wanted, though. You could see it on his face. Kyo waited through the next two *perfectly* thrown strikes.

Kyo waited till he saw the pitch that made him want to

swing. Till he knew he could bring Zuke home from third. He swung his bat, and we heard the crack, and the ball soared hard to left, bouncing just in front of the fielder. Everyone watched as Zuke slid home. That left fielder tried to throw home to get Zuke out, but there was no question Zuke was safe, and the ump spread his arms wide anyway.

The dust rose high from the commotion, but you could still see that ump's arms open wide while Kyo ran across first, and Coach walked out on the field shaking hands. Papa stood taller than I'd ever seen, and the sun, it shined like a spotlight only on our field, while the yells from the crowd grew loud enough to make Kimi cover her ears, to make Mama laugh.

I don't know why, but I looked at Horse just then. I was walking on the field with the rest of my team, but I looked over at Horse, and I saw him smile like he might be making some room. That whatever was inside him too hard to say might let a red-orange fish move over. Might let a white fish come inside.

WE SENT THEIR team off after dinner, after a few of us tried sumo wrestling, to show them thank you for coming, and this is the sort of thing we do for fun around here.

We watched their yellow school bus drive away to a part of the free world.

I heard Kyo tell once more how the last inning went to his brother, then made my way back to the ball field.

I sat down and waited until the bats flew low over nearby bushes, until the sun slipped behind the Sacaton Mountains and the smell of sagebrush grew heavy.

I heard the yells from that afternoon in my mind. I saw Kyo hit the last pitch to left field and Zuke slide into home.

They made me believe in what *could* happen, and in a 125-acre fruit farm thirty-five miles south of where Lefty was.

I looked down at the dust that Mama had fought with her broom all this time, that had found its way to Kimi's lungs, that had been transformed into a ball field.

I picked up a handful of that dust and let it slip through my fingers.

I let it drift into the night air, and said my good-byes to Gila River. And just then, I felt happy because I'd been part of a team that gave me something that reminded me of home.

I knew one day I'd join a new team when we got back to California. I'd walk to practice that first day with my mitt, wondering where the coach would play me and what kind of hitters they had.

But first, I'd throw the ball to Lefty. I'd throw it as far as I could and watch him run to catch that ball, and it would, almost, be like before.

AUTHOR'S NOTE

The idea for this book began at a middle school National History Day competition. One of the students had built a model of the Zenimura baseball field as it stood outside Gila River for her project. I was fascinated by it. I asked her if I could interview her grandfather, who had played outfield on the team that beat the Arizona state champions back in 1945. I thought I would write a short article about him, but after the interview, I immediately called the pitcher and another member of the team to learn more. This began a two-year process of discovering everything I could about Gila River and the baseball team that came together, bringing hope and a sense of normalcy to the camp residents.

I spent many months at the Pacific Region Laguna Niguel National Archives Building reading through three and a half years of the *Gila News-Courier* on microfiche. The research attendant kindly ordered every roll from Washington, D.C., then showed me how to thread them through the machine. Each morning, I arrived as they opened, walked through the metal detector, then surrendered the last of my water bottle so I wouldn't accidentally ruin original documents or films. The attendants there are true professionals, knowing how to locate any piece of information one could ever want to read about.

The National Japanese American Historical Society in San Francisco has many publications that helped tremendously, specifically *Nikkei Heritage*, "The Big Lie: Japanese Evacuation from the West Coast" (Volume IV, Fall 1992).

California State University in Fullerton provided a collection of interviews with internees: the Japanese American Collection during Internment.

This book is a work of fiction based on newspaper articles and interviews with three players. Many events in this book—the young girl almost drowning, the fishponds, the tainted canal water, the competition to get pomegranates, the championship game against Tucson High School—really happened. According to the men I interviewed, their families went willingly to the internment camp, never complaining. It took a while for me to understand this, and to grasp what *gaman* meant. Simply, it is enduring the seemingly unbearable with patience and dignity.

For more information about Gila River and the baseball team, see:

Baseball-reference.com: http://www.baseball-reference.com/bullpen/ Kenichi_Zenimura

Burton, J., M. Farrell, F. Lord, and R. Lord. *Confinement and Ethnicity: An Overview of World War II Japanese American Relocation Sites.* Chapter 4: Gila River Relocation Center. *Publications in Anthropology 74,* 1999 (rev. July 2000): http://www.cr.nps.gov/history/online_books/ anthropology74/ce4.htm

Furukawa, Tetsuo. "When Gila Fought Heart Mountain": http://www .discovernikkei.org/en/journal/2010/2/26/nikkei-heritage/

"Gila River Relocation Center, Arizona," reproduced from *Echoes of Silence: The Untold Stories of the Nisei Soldiers Who Served in WWII:* http://www.javadc.org/gila_river_relocation_center.htm

Hirasuna, Delphine. *The Art of Gaman: Arts and Crafts from the Japanese American Internment Camps, 1942–1946.* Berkeley, California: Ten Speed Press, 2005.

Japanese American Baseball History Project: http://www.nikkeiheritage .org/research/bbhist.html

MLB.com

Nakagawa, Kerry Yo. *Through a Diamond: 100 Years of Japanese American Baseball.* San Francisco: Rudi Publishing, 2001.

National Japanese American Historical Society: http://www.njahs.org/

Singer, Tom. "Baseball Cast Light in Shadow of War": http://mlb.mlb .com/news/article.jsp?ymd=20080306&content_id=2408279&vkey =spt2008news&fext=.jsp&c_id=mlb

ACKNOWLEDGMENTS

In my home office are one thousand paper cranes. They are suspended by a sturdy string and strewn across from corner to corner, partially blocking the skylight and casting shadows onto my desk each late afternoon. The cranes were given to me as a gesture of good luck from Tetsuo Furukawa, to whom I owe a tremendous amount of gratitude for letting me interview him over the course of two years while I wrote this book. Now in his eighties, he still recalls almost every detail of his life while at Gila River, especially his time spent on the baseball field playing first base and pitching.

I also want to thank Jack Shosan Shimasaki and Howard Zenimura for letting me interview them as well. Along with Mr. Furukawa, they were part of the 1945 Butte High School Eagles baseball team. Mr. Zenimura was team captain and played second, while Mr. Shimasaki played outfield. Thank you also to Danley Shimasaki, his lovely granddaughter, and to Kerry Yo Nakagawa.

In addition, I am grateful to the staff at the Laguna Niguel National Archives branch for retrieving the *Gila News-Courier*—all nine rolls of microfiche—and for showing me how to work that old copy machine so I could take home the pages of the newspaper I needed most.

Carolyn Yoder at *Highlights for Children* magazine was the first to suggest I write this book. She helped me to write the best article I could for her magazine, then asked if I thought it could be a full-length book. Thank you—it turned out that it could be.

My SCBWI critique group—Lori Polydoros, Bev Plass, Nadine Fischel, Collyn Justis, and Nancy D'Aleo-Russey—gave unending support and advice. Thank you also to Jesper Widen, Alan Williams, and Ernesto Cisnero.

Thank you to Paul Angle, my son's former Little League baseball coach, who provided immeasurable assistance and long, detailed explanations about the game of baseball, including what each player in the field would be thinking and doing in certain situations and innings. He grew up a Phillies fan, but these days, you can find him at most of the Angels' home games.

Thank you also to Patrick Diamond for technical advice, for reading every baseball scene after school that day (even though he had tons of homework), and for explaining to me how it feels to play catch in the dust. He's a Yankees fan, which tells you all you need to know.

Jennifer Rofe remains the very best literary agent a writer could hope for. She is there always, from the first sentence to the twentieth revision, never ever letting go of my hand, which means the world to me.

Thank you to Janet Pascal and Susan G. Jeffers for polishing everything up so perfectly.

And, above all, thank you to Catherine Frank, whose brilliant editing transformed this story into something much better than I ever could have imagined. I am so very grateful for her guidance and wisdom, and for helping me to understand the ending.